Andrea Meneghini

POPULANA
A world without heroes

Translated by
Fiona Grace Peterson

Andrea Meneghini

ISBN: 9781073114962

This book is dedicated to those who are mistrustful of their fellow men.

INDEX

1. THE CALL	1
2. DESTINY	3
3. TETRON	6
4. CHARLIE	10
5. EPIPHANY	14
6. CHOICE	17
7. FAREWELL	19
8. ZIMDAR	21
9. MANDEO	25
10. MARIANNE	32
11. SERENDIPITY	36
12. KOSTAS	39
13. LAW	42
14. OUTAGE	46
15. MEV	52
16. CHANDAHA	55
17. LATROPP	58
18. WAR	66
19. FAITH	69
20. KAREN	72
21. FANDAR	75
22. JOE	77
23. DOUBT	84
24. LIGHT	86
25. KARMA	89
26. SURPRISE	92
27. RAZOR	94
28. ABYSS	101
29. SARA	104

30. HONESTY	111
31. REVELATION	113
32. WAKEUP	118
33. CONSPIRACY	122
34. ORTIEP	129
35. JUSTICE	134
36. TRUTH	139
37. STORM	146
38. BROTHERHOOD	152
39. TIM	155
40. MORA	158
41. TOM	161
42. KURMAR	163
43. VIRUS	170
44. LIGHTNING	175
45. THUNDER	178
46. IMPULSE	183
47. TRUST	187
48. POPULANA	191
49. RESURRECTION	201
50. FREEDOM	204
51. HEROES	207

1. THE CALL

Ariel Nat was furious.

Who were they to decide his future? What gave them the right? They sure knew how to pick their moment, just when he'd found a job and a girlfriend, all in one fell swoop, after all the blood, sweat and tears. The gorgeous Marianne Giltor - what a piece of luck meeting her right before the interview. The best day of his life.

His expectations up to then had all been shattered in a maze of slammed doors, and his self-esteem had hit rock bottom when that lardball at Kurmar Enterprise had dismissed him with that greasy smirk; alright, so he was just a kid and didn't have much going for him, but it sure seemed as if the world had made up its mind that there was no place for him in it anywhere.

But that morning, when that delicate chestnut hair had appeared like a picture frame around that enchanting smile, Ariel had smelled the change in the air, almost like a good omen, a delicious perfume.

And as if by magic, everything had begun to go his way.

He could still remember his surprise when, after not even fifteen minutes of interview, those gratifying words of congratulation had erased all those frustrating months and endless rounds of "Don't call us, we'll call you..."

It had taken a while to sink in: Razor, one of the biggest corporations in all of Populana, undisputed leader in the information and technology sector, had decided to hire him.

And it was then that his life had really begun to change. It had only been a few months, but he was doing well at the office: he enjoyed the work, and could afford the rent of a great little apartment near the center of Novardia.

But the best thing was the splendid Marianne, fast asleep by his side, breathing lightly, the picture of tranquility.

He lingered a moment, watching her, hypnotized by that nightdress softly rising and falling to the imperceptible music of her dreams.

He longed to dive in to that sea of tenderness, but he held back. At the bottom of his heart, he knew that waking her up would make this nightmare even more real than it already was.

The Call. Why him? Why right now?

He certainly couldn't refuse. No-one would understand. Work...relationships...his whole life would go to hell. And yet he couldn't get his head around it: what contribution could he possibly make, so young and inexperienced, in the rooms of power?

It was sheer madness.

2. DESTINY

He woke the next morning exhausted, as if he'd barely slept half an hour. It was 7:30, and Marianne must have just got up, the mattress still showing the faint trace of her silhouette.

"And what a silhouette…" murmured Ariel, proudly tracing that ephemeral shape with his fingers.

As he turned his face to the light filtering into the room, he felt a gentle throbbing in his temples. Not a good sign: staying in bed would inevitably bring that same inexplicable pounding headache as always. He would feel better if he got up, and that thought alone made him throw back the covers.

"Damned walls won't stay still," muttered Ariel, swaying his way along the corridor like a drunk.

In the kitchen, Marianne was already having breakfast. How she managed to be so fresh-faced having just woken up was one of life's mysteries - the girl clearly had coffee in her veins.

But if he was honest, her reaction the night before had disappointed him. Deep down, he had hoped for some sign of anger at the news, searching her eyes for some sign of solidarity, complicity for an epic battle against everything and everyone, but found none.

Marianne had taken the news calmly, almost too calmly, as if it was some inevitable fate she had been expecting. "After all, we've got our whole lives ahead of us. A year's not that long. It'll be over before we know it." Those had been her words. But it would be a year far away from her, and the mere thought of not being able to hold her in his arms made him feel positively ill.

And Ariel had absolutely no intention of putting his career on hold. Of course his desk would be waiting for him when he got back, but think of all the opportunities he would miss. Not to mention the thought of that idiot Charlie Baid being promoted before him.

In any case, the way his father had yelled at him with the typical tact of a freshly-branded steer had left him no choice. "Why not go hang out with the smackheads while you're at it? Because if you turn down the Call, people are gonna avoid you like some two-bit junky, and the people you stay behind for'll be the first to turn their back on you. If that good girl Marianne had wanted a doormat, she'd have gone to the hardware store!"

To Ariel it was hypocrisy, pure and simple: he was convinced that, above and beyond what they taught at school, abandoning your life and everything in it to go and play politics was beyond reasonable for pretty much anyone. Sheer idiocy, that's what it was. A taboo that couldn't be broken, just because some clown had decided that was how things should be.

"If only people weren't such slaves to convention," he thought bitterly, "we could all live our lives however the hell we wanted."

Lost in his misery, he was completely unaware of having started breakfast with Marianne's chocolate biscuits. "You are gonna leave me some, right?" she asked him, with that amused pout that got him every time.

By way of response, he pulled her close, and as her soft warmth spread through his chest, he decided he would do whatever it took to avoid losing what he had fought so hard for: he would go to the Tetron that very same day for the Acceptance.

He still had no idea where that decision would take him.

3. TETRON

The Tetron of Novardia stood at the top of a grassy rise in the city's main square.

The last time Ariel had set foot in the huge pyramid had been during the sixth-grade school trip. To be honest, he didn't remember much about that day, having spent all his time playing with his friend Markus, the only way to beat the deathly boredom of that interminable outing.

But now, as he came through the entrance, Ariel realized he should have paid more attention to what they'd been taught that day.

Just then he remembered that series of huge inscriptions, explaining step-by-step what the Chosen One had to do, right down to the smallest detail. He was intrigued by the fact that in this technological era, the country had decided to carve the instructions on stone, but this minor quirk paled in comparison to the enigma of the Fourth Room.

The founding fathers had taken every precaution to ensure no-one would discover what was at the heart of those pyramids that formed the nodes of the Great Network, the country's operative intelligence and the archive of the entire society.

The central room of the complex, devoid of any openings whatsoever, was shaped during construction by the special Modelbyte robots used to build the Tetrons, a procedure that, on closer inspection, wasn't so different from that used to build houses.

Each building started life as a large block of Forgez, a material that could be shaped using different types of radiation. Once the preparatory phase was complete, the Modelbyte robots interacted with the material to create the interiors and exteriors of the building, according to the project they had been programmed to execute.

The main difference was that the powerful radio-controlled variants of the standard Modelbyte used for the Tetrons, known as T0s, remained inside the fourth room once construction was complete. The T0s used a top-secret communication protocol developed by the founding fathers, that no-one had ever been able to crack.

The founding of a new city began with the building of a hillock and the positioning of a cube of Forgez on top. On construction day, the other Tetrons of Populana transmitted in unison, sending the project for the pyramid to the new T0 robots.

The flow of data also contained the mysterious specifications of the Fourth Room, but no-one had ever been able to decipher it. In over 300 years of history, there wasn't the slightest hint that the system had ever failed, or that someone had managed to interfere with the immense network.

For Ariel, not knowing what was in the central

room was more than mere curiosity: ever since he was a child, he had had the ominous sensation that something terrible was hiding behind those walls.

Brushing these thoughts aside, he carried on timidly through the first of the three rooms which formed a U-shape around the mysterious center of the building.

The Gaudion machine took up the entire wall of the Chamber of Equality, vast and unmoving, like a gigantic bear in hibernation, waiting for the beauty of spring. At the center of the large screen, in colossal digits, was a number, surrounded by dates and other smaller numbers.

That number, that 10647758 written in huge figures, was the same one tattooed on Ariel's arms, neck and abdomen: the identity number he had been assigned by the Tetrons at his baptism shortly after birth. The numbers were impressed on his skin with a special nanobot-based ink, and these miniscule automatons formed a circuit that emitted a signal in response to a specific stimulus.

As he approached the enormous machine, Ariel heard a faint buzzing, and then, without warning, a niche appeared in the machine, exactly the same size and shape as his body.

Following the instructions on the inscription, he walked into the opening and waited. A dazzling light, a metallic hiss, a brief pause...then a friendly voice spoke. "Welcome Ariel Nat. Please continue through to the Chamber of Brotherhood."

Ariel obeyed the machine's words and stepped out of the niche.

The next room was dwarfed by a herculean inscription reading 'Brotherhood' on the right, in the same style as its counterpart 'Equality' in the previous room. On the opposite side was a large Kurmar VR chair and an inscription that invited him to take a seat.

The VR chair was similar to the one he used at home for gaming, with elegant red fabric trim and comfortable black armrests.

"Nothing new so far," thought Ariel. Kurmar VR chairs had been part of daily life in Populana for centuries, even though - to the great dismay of the manufacturers - their use had been limited by law to just three hours a day.

In the beginning, in fact, some people had proved completely incapable of distinguishing the virtual world from the real one, and there had been at least one case of someone dying because they had stayed in the chair for more than forty-eight hours. Those images of Vera Cloy, her lifeless body with that blissful smile, had provoked a whole range of reactions, but everyone agreed that such a senseless death should never be allowed to happen again.

Ariel was surprised by just how much he felt at home in the chair: like meeting an old friend and rediscovering that familiar sense of complicity that made the relationship so special.

With a gentle hum, the antenna with its six elements arranged in a hexagon positioned itself at the nape of his neck. It was time for him to visit the virtual world into which the machine would take him.

4. CHARLIE

A woman's voice began counting slowly backwards "Three, two, one...". Soon Ariel felt that familiar sense of relaxation: his eyelids growing heavier, his eyes beginning to close, a gentle caress on his forehead, the sound of his own breathing, then silence. Suddenly, a crescendo of voices and an irresistible desire to open his eyes... and there was Zico, his little toy dinosaur and constant companion during his work at Razor.

It was a day like any other, and Ariel had just finished sending his plan for the rewriting of routine 4357 of the network code, modifications designed to solve the sluggishness of the operating system and dramatically improving the users' experience of Razor, 'the personal assistant no self-respecting man should be without'.

It was lunchtime. "Better eat something," he thought, heading out of the office.

Wednesday was his favorite day, the day the canteen served its legendary meatballs and spaghetti. But when he spotted his boss Toss Sterling sitting with Charlie Baid, Ariel felt his hunger evaporate.

Gazing dismally at his plate, for a moment he was tempted to go and eat elsewhere. But his curiosity got the better of him and he sat down nearby, close enough to eavesdrop but far enough away that they wouldn't notice him.

The two were talking about the fluctuations in sales over the last two trimesters, and Charlie was arguing, in that slimeball smartass way of his, that adding flashy graphics would improve the experience of the end user.

But if the support tickets were anything to go by, Ariel was convinced the problem was caused by the Razor's network code, responsible for massive system slowdowns that eclipsed the device's true potential.

If he was right, Charlie's suggestion would only aggravate the problem, putting the quantum processor under even more stress. And judging from Toss's approving expression, there was a strong chance that Charlie was pushing all the right buttons, and that the development department would soon be taking him up on those ludicrous suggestions.

The worst thing was that if Charlie's idea got the go-ahead, the solution proposed by Ariel - the one he had worked on for months - would be relegated to the sidelines. Not only could he see his chances at promotion slipping away, he would also have to struggle to implement a strategy that was nothing short of suicide.

He stopped for a moment to observe the wretched strands of spaghetti, writhing like wounded snakes under the tortured twisting of his fork. "Maybe I should eat," he thought. "I'll deal with this problem later."

Devouring the contents of his plate as if it were his last meal before battle, he hurried out of the canteen to avoid having to listen to any more of that pitiful farce.

Returning to his desk, the office was still deserted. As he felt the first twinge of heartburn, it dawned on him that in his anger at Toss and Charlie, he'd shoveled his lunch down without chewing. Again. Not to mention cutting a good fifteen minutes off his break.

Walking over to his desk, Ariel couldn't help but notice, for the umpteenth time, the repulsive wallpaper splashed across Charlie's screen. "How the hell can anyone put a photo like that on their workstation?" he thought in disgust. Looking out at him was DJ Tarmac, idol of prepubescent girls. But with his gold necklace and surrounded by extremely attractive, scantily-clad women, he looked less like a musician and more like a pimp snapped as he collected his takings for the night.

"Gross," he thought, he shook his head in disgust. "What an insult to evolution! Not to mention you can barely see the desktop icons..."

"Hang on a sec…" He stopped, incredulous. "No way! That idiot's forgotten to log out! Anyone could get access to the code he's working on. How careless! Someone might just decide to play a little prank…".

Ariel glanced around the office. Everyone was still at lunch, and it wouldn't take much to teach Charlie a lesson. Cut him down to size.

Toss, in the canteen, had seemed pretty keen. "I don't have a choice," Ariel told himself. "I have to do something, or months of hard work will go down the drain because of that loser… not to mention the risks for the company."

He started towards Charlie's desk, but it was as if there was an invisible force pushing him back. He tried again, more forcefully this time, but it was no use.

He couldn't understand it: it was as if his body was refusing to obey the orders of his brain.

Why couldn't he move? What was stopping him? Something was wrong…

Everything happened in an instant: there were voices behind him and Charlie's workstation exploded in a blinding flash. Then darkness, an alarm ringing, shouting, jolts of electricity, followed once more by silence and blackness.

5. EPIPHANY

More than the exhortations of the paramedics, it was the vague pain in his neck and the stink of burnt quantum processor that brought Ariel round, taking him back to that time one of the engineers at Razor had had a little too much to drink, nearly setting the whole department on fire.

The power came back on just when his eyes were finally getting accustomed to the red of the emergency lights, although it was another few minutes before the white veil lifted from his field of vision.

In the meantime, the paramedics had been able to examine him: nothing serious, apart from a hexagonal burn on the back of his neck where the antenna had been.

The old custodian of the Tetron was incredulous: in all his years on the job, he'd never seen anything like it.

And with good reason: the Kurmar VR chairs were manufactured in accordance with the strictest quality control standards in the country, and those in the Tetrons were some of the most closely monitored in all of Populana.

The Test of Brotherhood was nothing too demanding: all the candidate had to do was to experience first-hand what their choices, dictated by their own interests, signified for others.

Normally, during the first phase of the experiment, the candidate was persuaded to do something that was detrimental to another person, for their own good or for that of the community, while the second part of the test required them to put themselves in their victim's shoes, to experience the consequences of their actions.

The exercise only lasted a few hours, but for the candidate in their virtual reality, it could seem like days. Although this type of compression was not new to the users of the VR chairs, there was a physical limit dictated by the machine and by the user's brain.

Even so, there had never been an instance of the experience ending like that after just a few minutes, at least as far as anyone could remember.

Arriving almost immediately, the Kurmar technicians declared the problem to be the unfortunate coincidence of an energy surge and an extremely rare quantum processor anomaly.

It didn't take long for the chair to be repaired, but since the results of the test were not binding, it was decided to save Ariel any more stress, and to allow him to go forward to the next stage.

And so it was that Ariel, picking up his own Razor which had somehow fallen off during the accident, stepped over the threshold of the Chamber of Freedom.

The curious event made the headlines for a while,

but was soon overshadowed by an increasing concern for the ever-more frequent power outages.

6. CHOICE

The Chamber of Freedom was similar to the previous rooms.

Emblazoned on the perimeter wall was a large inscription reading 'Freedom', visible from every corner of the room, while on the opposite side was a console with two red buttons, identical in every way apart from the words 'Accept' and 'Refuse' that distinguished the two. High up on the wall above the console was a large screen with the usual number, 10647758, in large digits.

Despite having spent all last night thinking about it, that moment was very different from how Ariel had imagined it. For some obscure reason, he felt compelled to press 'Accept', a decision that - just hours before - would have seemed impossible.

For a moment, looking at the two buttons, Ariel felt his life flash before his eyes: not knowing where that choice would take him was utterly terrifying.

What would become of his job, his loved ones, his comfortable routines?

He didn't have an answer, but now, standing there, it was as if he had always known he would press that button. And when he did, a shiver of excitement ran through him from head to toe.

7. FAREWELL

The magnetic levitation monorail sped towards the capital, the cultivated fields whipping from one window to the next, the snowy peaks in the distance passing at a more leisurely pace.

It had all happened so quickly: the press of that button had triggered a whirlwind of events that in a blink of an eye had whisked him onto the seat of that train.

After having received that silly medallion now dangling around his neck, Ariel had gone home, where he had read the affectionate note Marianne had hung on his suitcase.

Although they had said goodbye to each other properly the night before, that handwritten note had the nagging taste of farewell, an uncomfortable sensation that had accompanied him to the platform, following him on to the train despite his best efforts.

Ariel pushed the thoughts away and turned back to admire the view: "It's not so bad" he thought. "At least I'm travelling free for once!"

He glanced down at his hands fiddling with the medallion, remembering his surprise at the importance wearing that symbol had given him, the other passengers in the queue letting him go to the front when they noticed it. Perhaps that piece of metal with its stylized pyramid did have some use after all, although he knew that what really counted was the number on his arm.

Overcome by the tiredness he had accumulated over the preceding days, these thoughts turning over in his brain, Ariel dozed off on the seat of the train as it whistled across the plains of Populana.

8. ZIMDAR

His arrival in the capital Allesia was anything but thrilling. No buxom girls with flowers and bottles of champagne, no cheering crowd awaiting him. Just a decrepit old man with a medallion identical to his own.

"Jeez, he's ancient!" thought Ariel, looking him up and down.

If old age had had a face, it would have been that of Zimdar Kun. With every deliberate word that left his lips, the wrinkles on his brow would ripple like waves, foaming into his eyebrows as white as bones. As if that wasn't enough, his eyes, blue as the South Seas, were so small and piercing it was often difficult to hold his gaze.

Zimdar, the only citizen ever to be called twice to represent the nation, never wasted words. The long pauses that always preceded his replies were the object of much hilarity in the corridors of the High Chamber. Nevertheless, many couldn't wait for the two-week handover period to be over, so they no longer had to hear the ominous rhythm of his cane echoing through the building.

"Welcome young tyro, the old man greeted him, trying to catch Ariel's gaze.

Ariel averted his eyes and muttered "Thanks", before waiting interminable seconds for the old man to reply. "Come, young tyro, I will show you the way."

The two began walking towards the large complex which housed the High Chamber of Populana.

The circular four-story building stood on a rise in the center of Allesia, once the site of an ancient acropolis.

The lodgings of the High Representatives were located around the perimeter of the complex, with restaurants, shops and recreation areas on each floor of the building to meet their essential needs, while the hall used for debates and voting was in the center.

First, Zimdar took him to his assigned lodgings to let him settle in.

Ariel immediately recognized his identification number on the door, and watched in stupor as it clicked open when he reached towards it.

Although not particularly big, the apartment seemed very comfortable, with a large French window leading out on to a balcony, giving a splendid view over Allesia. There was a kitchenette and a dining table, and a couch separating the kitchen from the lounge with its Kurmar VR chair. The bedroom was spacious, with a double bed, which despite being fairly plain, looked exceedingly comfortable, and a cozy little en-suite bathroom decorated in relaxing colors.

"Not bad at all!", thought Ariel, feeling his mood begin to lift as he began to savor his night's rest, an idyll that was quickly shattered when old Zimdar informed him of the seven o'clock start the next morning. "Young tyro," he explained, "time is tight, and I have a lot to teach you in these two weeks. Make sure you are ready when I arrive."

"Stupid old fart" thought Ariel. "What the hell is he thinking? Seven in the morning is sleep o'clock, and after all the stress of the last few days, I really need to rest".

He was about to speak, but it was as if Zimdar had read his mind, shooting him a withering glance that extinguished the words in his mouth as fast as a match struck in a storm.

"Young tyro," the old man growled, "you have been given a wonderful opportunity. Do not waste it."

"Great," thought Ariel sourly, "this moldy old codger can read my mind too. As if I was the one who wanted all this…".

Once again, Zimdar seemed to know exactly what he was thinking. "In life, everything happens for a reason. But that reason does not always fit with what we want. We men are born as animals, but what makes us intelligent beings is the meaning we give to what happens to us. It is not our problems that make us what we are, but how we react to them. Rest now, my young tyro. Tomorrow will be a long day, for you *and* for me."

Absorbed as he was in trying to think of an intelligent response to shove in that old relic's face, Ariel was completely unaware that the old man had already left, and found himself saying goodbye to a closed door.

He felt his irritation rise, as always happened when he couldn't think of a witty remark in a conversation.

Lying in bed, he began mulling over all the things he could have said to put that old know-it-all in his place, before his anger gave way to sleep.

9. MANDEO

The next morning, Ariel was woken at seven by an incessant ringing breaking into his lucid dream about the enchanting Marianne.

He had spent the last half hour seducing her in a brazen attempt to get her into bed, and now that he was almost there, every time he caressed her naked skin, there it was. That damned ringing. And the more he caressed her, the more insistent it became.

Something wasn't right, and Ariel's mind slowly crossed over that subtle threshold separating illusion from reality.

He reached out to switch the alarm clock off, fingers meeting nothing but the smooth surface of the nightstand.

"What the hell...?" he wondered, turning over in bed. "It must be the door."

He reluctantly got out of bed and dragged himself across the room, only to find old Zimdar with his finger glued to the doorbell, presumably to the delight of the neighbors.

"You do not seem to be taking your mission very seriously, young tyro," the old man reproached him, observing the tousled figure in the doorway.

"Damned tyrant," thought Ariel. "Doesn't he have anything better to do than torture me in the middle of the night? There should be a law against this kind of thing."

"You have forty-five minutes to have breakfast and get ready," the old man told him, handing him some milk and a packet of cookies. "I brought you these."

The unexpected kindness of his gesture temporarily softened Ariel's anger, already shaping itself into various atrocious means of getting rid of this ball and chain he had suddenly been lumbered with.

Breakfast, although hurried, did him good, and as often happened, the simple act of putting food in his belly improved his mood.

When he had finished, their first port of call was the Great Hall.

More than a chamber, it resembled a small stadium, the high-backed chairs alternating on each level without interruption, and at the center, where the arena would be in an amphitheater, was the rotating platform used by the moderator.

It was so early that the hall was deserted, and Zimdar showed Ariel the seat that had been his the year before.

"Now," he lectured, indicating the place where Ariel would sit in the weeks to come, "a lot of people have given everything for you to be able to fill this position, and many others will suffer if you do not honor the reasons they did it for…"

"Maybe they've made a mistake!" Ariel interrupted boldly. "I'm just a kid! A computer programmer… I don't know anything about politics! I didn't even want to come here!"

Zimdar looked at him, frowning, but Ariel ploughed on. "Seriously, I'm just an ordinary person. I'm nothing special! This seat should be occupied by someone more suitable, someone able to make decisions…"

"And in a democracy, who do you think should choose this person?" asked his mentor with a roguish smile.

Still riding the wave of his previous logic, Ariel replied, "People could choose their representatives by voting…"

"Foolishness!" The old man laughed. "How can a population of ordinary people, as unworthy and incapable as you seem to think, select worthy and capable people by way of free elections? That is precisely the type of reasoning that led to the Great War, and I am amazed a youngster of Populana shares this same logic.".

Ariel reddened as he would always do when his teacher found out he hadn't studied, but just as back then, he wasn't about to give up without a fight. "But it's reasonable to assume that only the best individuals would be able to convince a large number of people to vote for them. Those candidates would be the embodiment of the very best our society has to offer, and as stupid as they might be, it's unlikely people would make too bad a choice."

Zimdar remained in silence, furrowing his thick eyebrows, and tightening his grip on his cane.

Bolder now, Ariel went on. "As long as we've been on this Earth, people have needed leaders and heroes to inspire them. Without a guide, we're nothing but sheep without a shepherd. And what contribution can

I possibly make? I didn't even want to come! Selecting our representatives by drawing lots is crazy - do you know how many stupid, bad, just plain *dumb* people there are out there? Just think, for example, if that boneheaded colleague of mine Charlie Baid was here in my place. Now *that* I'd like to see!" Ariel concluded, bursting into laughter.

The old man did not react, and gazed at him for a while, with such an intensity Ariel almost felt transparent.

Luckily, that embarrassing moment was interrupted by the most influential member of the High Chamber of Populana. Young and good-looking, with glossy black hair and a flawless complexion that betrayed the diligent attentions of a beautician, Mandeo Gutt had overheard the entire conversation, just waiting for the right moment to butt in.

"Looks like you've met your match, Zimdar old man!" he said, in the typical accent of the Quar region. "It's about time that seat went to someone who knows what's what!"

Ariel immediately recognized that voice he had heard several times on the evening news.

With the gift of the gab and never at a loss for a comeback, Mandeo - now halfway through his mandate - had built up a reputation that was entirely unheard of in the political history of Populana. Although political groups were forbidden in the High Chamber, he had succeeded in building up a small army of loyal followers who hung on his every word. His speeches in the House were often followed by riotous uproar, and although he never explicitly courted votes, his words always smacked of someone on a never-ending campaign trail. The media quickly cottoned on to his success, nominating him spokesman of the High Representatives, and barely a day went by that he didn't make an appearance.

Zimdar didn't bat an eyelid and remained with his gaze resting on Ariel, as if there was no-one else around.

"My young tyro," he said, after an interminable moment of reflection, "democracy is based on choices, and every choice is born from a free exchange of ideas. An idea is valid if any person can make it their own by way of reasoning. This mechanism fails, however, when people stop thinking for themselves and begin considering ideas based on who proposes them. The principle of authority, the absurd belief that there are individuals so brilliant that they never make a mistake, is the death of intelligent thought and of democracy."

He paused and then went on. "Ideas belong to everyone, and to allow everyone to consider them for what they are, no-one should ever label them with their name. And so, my young tyro, have faith in ideas, but always be wary of those who try to take their place. In life you will learn to recognize those who act in their own interests - such individuals are precisely those leaders who stamp their name on ideas, exploiting them to increase their own power."

Mandeo made to reply, but Zimdar ignored him. "Society, like the jungle, tends always to choose the strongest people. But the strongest person is not necessarily the most suited to pursuing the common good. On the contrary, the strongest is often he who is generous only with himself, the fat kitten who drinks the milk of his brothers and sisters... These people - narcissistic, selfish, sometimes sociopathic, are the least suited to governing on behalf of others," he concluded, inclining his head slightly in Mandeo's direction.

Old Zimdar resumed his discourse surprisingly quickly once more. "I know it might seem strange, but I was young once too, and like you, I had my doubts. I am sure that being torn away from your life and your loved ones was very painful for you. Sheep do not flock together out of choice, but to protect themselves from wolves. And that is why, for the sake of democracy, the citizens of Populana must willingly accept the duties that Fate has assigned them."

The clock struck nine.

Mandeo burst into one of his fits of laughter. "Good going, Zimdar old boy, now you're raving about sheep and wolves! I have to go, but let me know when I can catch the next episode of Little Red Riding Hood, so I can bring you a pillow, a blanket and a cup of hot tea!"

"Bye kid," he added, "it was a pleasure to meet you. If you ever want a serious conversation, you know where to find me."

And he turned on his heels and left.

Ariel's mind was elsewhere: all that talk of his life and his loved ones had reminded him of the beautiful Marianne.

"Dammit," he thought, "in all this chaos I've completely forgotten to call her. She must be worried, or mad at me...".

As per usual, Zimdar seemed to know exactly what he was thinking. "Go on, young tyro," he murmured, "do what you must..."

Thanking him, Ariel hurried away, without even noticing the old man's cane which had fallen out of his hands and was rolling down the steps. Zimdar's eyes followed the hexagonal mark on Ariel's neck, until it was nothing more than a vague shadow in his mind.

10. MARIANNE

As soon as he got back to the apartment, Ariel rushed to his suitcase for his personal assistant.

Slim as a razor blade but soft to the touch, the Razor was a flexible device similar to an adhesive label, which could be placed on any part of the body. Some people wore it on the back of their hand, some on their forearm, others in places where the sun never shone.

The surface in contact with the skin was perhaps one of the craziest inventions of the last few years, conceived when a nanotechnology laboratory technician, waking up on a semi-deserted beach after a night of heavy drinking, had observed a small reptile climb on to a slippery rock to await the first rays of sun.

Breaking practically every animal protection law in existence, the guy first got the hapless animal drunk then kidnapped it to study it in the laboratory, efforts which culminated in the invention of a material that could stick to any surface on command.

To his great misfortune, however, the researcher

didn't have time to enjoy the fruits of his labors, dragged almost immediately to court by animal rights activists. The poor Gui Nes was sentenced before he could patent his invention, to the delight of the big corporations such as Razor, now able to use Reptiflex without fear of reprisal.

The unfortunate reptile, tame by now, fared no better. Taken back to its native island, it was immediately wolfed down by an enormous predator, under the horrified gaze of the handful of animal rights activists who had set it free it just moments before.

Ariel was rarely without his Razor, evident by the pale patch on his left forearm, and even wore it at night time, since body heat extended the device's battery life by several hours.

Grabbing his personal assistant, he remembered the strange sensation he had felt when coming round from his fulminating experience in the Tetron. For the first time in many years, his arm felt naked, and with it came an unexpected feeling of lightness, almost like a load had been taken off his mind.

In the confusion of the last few days, he had completely forgotten to put the Razor back on: strangely the display still read 2:56, the time the Kurmar VR chair had almost fried his brain.

At first Ariel thought the device was broken, but as soon as he brought it close to his body, the words 'Attach Me' appeared on the screen. Relieved, Ariel ran his finger over it and immediately felt that familiar grip, as if hundreds of tiny fingers were curling themselves around the fine hairs on his arm.

Immovable as a second skin, the Razor updated the display and said: "You have eleven missed calls, eight from Marianne and three from Father."

Ariel raised his forearm slightly and commanded: "Call Marianne."

The personal assistant seemed to freeze for a moment, just enough time for him to curse at the "damned slowdowns!!!", then a female voice announced the call and the device began beeping at regular intervals.

Marianne answered almost immediately. She was angry - no, *furious* - but relieved, that mixture of emotions when good news crushes the fear of just moments before.

"So you're alive!" she retorted. "Why didn't you call me before?"

"Sweetheart, I'm sorry, these days have just been crazy and I haven't had time... I even forgot to put on my Razor!"

"But you never take it off!" Marianne exclaimed.

"I know," he admitted, "but with the problems at the Tetron, the journey, and this crazy old mentor running me into the ground, I haven't had a moment's peace..."

"Didn't you think of me?"

"Of course I thought of you... I even dreamt about you!"

"You must have called me in your dreams then!", she said, sarcastic.

"Please don't be like that, Marianne, you're the first person I've called. I'm going to be up to my eyeballs in these two weeks of handover, but things will get better, I promise. But I've got to go because I still have to call my dad, I haven't called him yet either."

"Fine," she said with a touch of resignation. "But call as soon as you can."

"Sure! Bye gorgeous!"

The call that followed was shorter but no less intense: his father sure had a gift for brevity, and always managed to remind him of all his failings before he could even draw breath. Deep down, Ariel knew he wasn't a bad person, it was just his father's way of showing his love.

Ending the second call, his stomach reminded him it was time to go and get something to eat. Gulping down a glass of water, Ariel left the apartment and headed to the supermarket.

11. SERENDIPITY

The shops at the High Chamber of Populana were the same as the ones in the city. Customers walked through the aisles, scanning the product samples and selecting the quantity to purchase on the screen. At the checkout, they placed the reader in its housing and scan the identification number tattooed on their forearm to verify their identity. If the credit deposited in their name in the Tetron was sufficient, the groceries arrived neatly packed on a conveyor belt.

The only difference was that in the shops of the High Chamber, no money was subtracted from the High Representatives, up to a monthly maximum equivalent to the median wage of the workers of Populana. Indeed, the delegates did not receive a wage, and this system covered their essential needs.

Ariel immediately made his way into that maze of products, scanning this and that, paying attention to the price, the total weight of the groceries, and to the ingredients shown on the reader each time.

The Zanco chocolate cookies he left on the shelf,

which despite the obsessive advertising campaign assuring consumers of their goodness, contained various nasty ingredients at the very limits of legality. The same went for the Zin candies, where the sugar had been substituted with acevilriozanine, a chemical compound deriving from the waste generated during the production of pigments for industrial paints.

"Old Zimdar isn't so far off the mark after all," Ariel thought. "Some people would do anything to make money, and the more they trample on others, the richer and more powerful they become...".

Immersed as he was in his suspicions, Ariel almost collided with a girl rushing distractedly out of the frozen foods department, causing both of them to drop their readers. Ariel slipped on the damp floor, almost joining his reader on the ground.

"I'm so sorry!" Ariel gasped, his gaze yanked back to reality.

The woman looked like the classic girl next door, squeaky-clean, short hair framing a pretty face with very little makeup, and casual clothes that looked like they'd been made for her.

"Why don't you watch where you're going, Mister High Representative?" she snarled, her eye falling on his medallion.

"I'm so sorry, truly I am... my old mentor won't let me sleep, and I end up in a dream..."

"You nearly killed me!" she retorted. "Good dream, was it?"

"Sometimes reality is better..." he offered with a wink.

"Looks like someone's still in dreamland!", she fired back, grabbing her reader, and was gone before Ariel could come up with an intelligent reply.

The encounter had unsettled him, and returning to the apartment, he found himself thinking of the million ways he could have avoided making such an idiot of himself.

It was only when he got home and opened the grocery bags that he realized none of the items on the table were his. Tampons, Zanco cookies, tea, and even a package of the horrendous Tormu, a "health food" that tasted like goat dung.

"No, not Tormu! Unless I'm completely out of it, these aren't my groceries!" he thought. "That girl must have picked up the wrong reader!"

Now what? Not to mention he had no way of getting in touch with her.

"To hell with it, no way am I going back to the supermarket!" muttered Ariel, biting into the first Zanco cookie. "Just this once, I swear! I'll give up tomorrow…"

12. KOSTAS

After ingurgitating an insane number of cookies, Ariel decided to catch up on a bit of sleep, promising himself a real meal for dinner.

He'd been in bed for less than a minute when the doorbell rang again.

"Damned old slave driver, you're gonna drive me mad!" Ariel growled, dragging himself reluctantly to the door.

He was wrong: standing at the door was Mandeo with Kostas Bull, a greasy lardball who gave the impression of being his henchman.

"Come on in", said Ariel politely, inviting them to take a seat.

"Hey Ariel!" Mandeo greeted him enthusiastically. "I've come to give you my personal welcome, and to express my most sincere regret at you having to put up with that raving old loon of a mentor."

Ariel smiled, more out of politeness than agreement, while the minion grunted in approval at his boss.

Ariel's guest went on. "You see, even if I'm not your mentor, it's become a habit of mine to welcome all the new arrivals and make them feel at home. Although it looks to me that you're well on your way…", he said, winking in the direction of the box of tampons on the table with a sly grin.

"It's a long story…", replied Ariel, embarrassed, aware how childish his explanation would sound.

Mandeo smiled and went on. "Nothing to be ashamed about, *au contraire*! If you ever want some company, just let me know. Ask and you shall receive!!"

"Thanks, but…" Ariel began, before Mandeo cut him off. "I fear old Zimdar is filling your head with nonsense. Obsessed as he is with the Great War, he can't see the problems happening right here and now. The age he is, I'm surprised he can even see where he's going!" He laughed.

"You see, my dear Ariel, I'm extremely concerned about the economic crisis and about the discontent that a reckless management of Populana could bring about… Unfortunately our fathers, exhausted by the war, left us a system of government that's slow and inefficient. Every tiny decision requires infinite debates, and the constant turnover of High Representatives doesn't permit the development of the expertise necessary to make good decisions… the result is that young people like you are torn away from their lives for a career they're not prepared for. While those who - like me - would be prepared to sacrifice everything for the good of the nation, can only do so for one year, before being sent home with the enormous waste of the expertise they've accumulated…. I'm trying to change all of this for the good of us all. My dream is to give the people a chance to choose a class of professional politicians with the skill to do all those things that ordinary people aren't able to, or aren't interested in doing. Professionalism and governability are the new watchwords... It's not easy though; the rules of the game are practically set in stone, and I'm running out of time to change them. And that's why I'm hoping for your full support... If everything goes as planned, you'll soon be back in your old life with your loved ones, leaving this thankless task to someone else...".

His words were interrupted by the groaning creaks of the couch, barely able to withstand the bulk of Mandeo's hulking sidekick.

Ariel, who was beginning to feel a vague sense of repulsion for this huckster now sitting in his lounge, politely replied that it seemed like an awesome idea, before dropping heavy hints about the arrival of some fictitious guests.

Mandeo looked satisfied. "Good boy! Hang in there these two weeks with old Zimdar - he's so old he could be your great-great grandfather! Unfortunately, he was handed this second mandate when he was already suffering from senile dementia... One more reason to overhaul this system!" he concluded as he left, his lumbering colleague in tow.

13. LAW

Zimdar arrived later that afternoon to show him the work of the assembly.

Even though it would still be the old man voting that first week, Ariel felt strangely emotional: it was exciting to become part of something so important.

Before they went, he felt obliged to tell the old man about Mandeo's visit.

"My young tyro," Zimdar interrupted him calmly, "I am here to show you the way, not to hold your hand. You are an adult and you can spend your time with whoever you wish. All I ask is that you listen to what I tell you in these two weeks, and then make up your own mind. We should go."

Inside the large Chamber, they took their places to listen to the discussion, which concerned the electricity company, currently under public ownership. Mandeo Gutt, proposer of the law on the screen, proposed contracting the company out to private firms, which would solve the problem of the power outages.

As was obligatory in Populana, the text of the law was brief, and consisted of three simple points, the constitution having established precise rules by which laws were to be drawn up, besides setting out the fundamental principles of the nation and the structure of its institutions.

Every law had to meet various conditions: be numbered with the year of proposal and a progressive number, which returned to zero on the first day of each new calendar year; contain a maximum of three points, limited to 45 words each; be unique and uniform in its content; be logically coherent with all other laws in force, and contain a list of all the laws related to it in the large dependency tree.

Last but not least, the constitution required the laws to be written in a language that the whole population could understand. To guarantee this last point, one of the exams all high school seniors had to take consisted of a random selection of newly-passed laws, and the students had to identify which of the ten proposed scenarios violated the law in question. If more than 30% of Populana's students failed the test, the law was sent back to the Chamber to be rewritten within a month, or risk being annulled.

Looking at the screen on the desk, Ariel remembered his father's rage when he had failed one of those tests, and was glad those days were far behind him.

On the left of the monitor was the current version of the law:

(0001-140) ELECTRICAL GRID/001
1. The electrical grid is defined as the entire body of infrastructure used for the production and distribution of electrical energy for public and private purposes.

2. The electrical grid belongs to the State and may not be transferred to third parties.

3. The management of the electrical grid is entrusted to the State Electricity Company in accordance with the methods defined in <u>(0001-141) ELECTRICAL GRID/002.</u>

Related laws

↔ <u>(0001-141) ELECTRICAL GRID/002</u>

The numbering showed it was the 140th law promulgated during the first year following Populana's foundation.

On the right-hand side was Mandeo's proposal:

(0346-32) ELECTRICAL GRID/001

1. The electrical grid is defined as the entire body of infra-structure used for the production and distribution of electrical energy for public and private purposes.

2. The electrical grid belongs to the State and may not be transferred to third parties.

*3. The management of the electrical grid is entrusted to private companies by way of a public auction, established in accordance with the methods defined in <u>(0346-33)</u> <u>ELECTRICAL GRID/002.</u>

Proposer: Mandeo Gutt

Promulgation requires:

Approval of

↔ <u>(0346-33) ELECTRICAL GRID/002</u>

Abrogation of

! <u>(0001-140) ELECTRICAL GRID/001</u>

!↔! <u>(0001-141) ELECTRICAL GRID/002</u>

When Zimdar explained it to him, Ariel's first thought was that the procedure was rather pedantic: any modification not only required the entire individual law to be rewritten, but also the abrogation of the previous law.

But that wasn't all: the new law would only come into force if the High Chamber had also abrogated all those that depended on the old law, since they could not remain in force without a law of reference.

"Talk about nitpicking!" joked Ariel when the old man had finished talking. "I don't know how you all manage to stay awake in here!".

His mentor replied patiently "This system is necessary to respect the obligations established by the constitution. It also helps to maintain order, and forces each High Representative to pay close attention and not waste the only two bills they are allowed to propose during their mandate."

14. OUTAGE

The debate was about to begin, and Ariel could barely contain his excitement. Zimdar had pledged a lot of his remaining credits so he would have the right to speak.

The High Representatives, in fact, received a certain number of tokens every month giving them time to speak in the Chamber; the bids were secret, and only the fifteen highest bidders could take part. This was Populana's system, to guarantee that everyone had an equal chance to participate in the debates. But in this case, the proposer Mandeo had not needed to invest any credit.

"Mandeo versus Zimdar, what a duel!" Ariel thought. "Shame there's no popcorn… maybe a couple of nice sharp swords, that way maybe they'll run each other through and let me get a decent night's sleep!".

Mandeo spoke first, in his usual obsequious style. "Ladies and gentlemen, we are joined here to discuss an important bill aimed at improving the pitiful state of our infrastructure. The recent outages that have affected Populana, and our growing utility bills, show that public management of the electrical grid is inefficient, carried out by individuals without the necessary expertise to do a good job. While there are private companies which, with no help of any kind, have been able to make a profit from what to our State is an expenditure. This is the model we must follow, because greater efficiency means lower costs for all of us, and today's savings are tomorrow's freedom. For this, ladies and gentlemen, I am asking for your vote!"

Members all around the Chamber burst into raucous applause, while Mandeo returned theatrically to his seat.

The moderator coughed a couple of times and spoke in irritation. "Ladies and gentlemen, we have been over this before on several occasions. Approval is to be shown by voting, not by squawking like geese!"

A number of other members spoke, putting forward more or less complex arguments, until it was the turn of Zimdar, who had been observing the scene impassive up to then. "Sisters and brothers, High Representatives of the Republic of Populana, the management of our energy systems is of paramount importance for the survival of our democracy. Ever since the dawn of time, energy has distinguished civilization from barbarity. Energy is the food we eat, the water we drink: it is the power that warms our homes, it is our work, our leisure. Energy is our freedom, it is also our democracy, that shines from the Tetrons in all the cities of Populana. Energy belongs to everyone, in equal measure. The distribution network cannot be managed for profit, it must stay public and neutral.

So, it is with my heart, but above all with my head, that I ask you to reje…"

Amplified by speakers, Zimdar's voice suddenly cut out, plunging the Chamber into a surreal silence, the end of his sentence heard only by those sitting nearby. The screens and the lights went out in unison, the light seeming to follow the old man's voice into some mysterious, faraway place.

A hum of voices rose in the Chamber as quickly as silence had fallen: it was the second episode in a week, highly unusual for Populana where, with the exception of the last few months, you could count the number of outages on the fingers of one hand.

The outage did not last long, and the power was restored before the auxiliary generators kicked in.

The moderator tapped on the microphone to make sure it was working. "Ladies and gentlemen, order please! All this confusion seems rather unnecessary for a mere power cut! The session is adjourned for fifteen minutes, the time necessary to verify that all systems are operative…"

Ariel looked at Zimdar with a quizzical air.

The old man seemed to know what he was thinking. "I do not know the cause, young tyro, but I can imagine the effect it will have, and it does not help our cause. I fear there is little hope for us at this point."

"Do you think this law will cause problems for Populana?" asked Ariel hesitantly.

"It already has done in the past, my young tyro, it already has," sighed Zimdar, before withdrawing into silence.

Ariel's gaze wandered around the hall. There was a bit of everything going on: some Representatives had left to go to the bathroom or to make a phone call, some were consulting the news to see if the event had already made the headlines, while others were simply dozing.

In all that assortment of human activity, Ariel couldn't help but notice Mandeo's pleased expression, while a handful of High Representatives led by Kostas was congratulating him as if he had already won his battle.

"Please take your seats, ladies and gentlemen, the session will now resume!" commanded the moderator shortly afterwards, waiting for the latecomers to arrive before he continued. "The State Electrical Company has informed me that the outage was caused by a power surge throughout the whole of Populana. The technicians have not been able to pinpoint its origin, since it does not seem to have occurred in a specific area. They have also informed me that although energy production has been increased three times in the last two months, the intensity of the surges has also increased, therefore the occurrence of further outages cannot be ruled out. The investigation is still underway."

"Returning to the discussion of (0346-32), I believe High Representative Zimdar Kun has expressed his opinion fully…" he added, pausing for confirmation.

The old man nodded, and the moderator went on. "Very well, that was the final contribution. Voting will be open for the next 15 minutes."

Ariel looked at his mentor in dismay. "If you really believe it's that important, why didn't you ask to finish what you were saying?"

Zimdar turned to him and replied "That which

had to be said has been said. Nothing I could add would change what has just happened. Sadly, a falling tree makes more noise than a growing forest… The future of Populana is now in the hands of the High Representatives, and we must have faith in them. Always remember: democracy is synonymous with trust."

And with that, he brought his identification number close to the reader, and touched the desk screen twice on the red 'NO' button.

Time flew by, and the moderator solemnly announced the results. "Voters 355, abstentions 0, in favor 192, against 163. The High Chamber of Populana approves!"

The Chamber exploded in vigorous applause just as swiftly as it was silenced by the powerful voice of the moderator. "Ladies and gentlemen, *please*!"

Voting for (0346-33) ELECTRICAL GRID/002 followed with the same result.

The moderator announced: "Let us now proceed with the voting for the abrogation of (0001-140) ELECTRICAL GRID/001. You have fifteen minutes to reserve your places in the debate and to consult the text on your screens. May I remind you that the abrogation of this law is necessary for the approval of the previous proposals, and that we are also voting to abrogate all laws correlated to the one now under discussion."

No-one asked to speak and the voting was over quickly, but with a result that was anything but foreseen, since some Representatives had decided to vote against the bill instead of in favor.

"Voters 355, abstentions 0, in favor 180, against 175. The High Chamber of Populana abrogates!"

Zimdar was still hopeful: indeed, there was one last chance to prevent Mandeo's proposal being approved. If (0001-141) ELECTRICAL GRID/002 remained in force, so would all correlated laws, and the new law would be scrapped.

But the illusion was short-lived, even though a shiver ran down Mandeo's spine when the moderator announced: "Voters 355, abstentions 1, in favor 178, against 176. The High Chamber of Populana abrogates!"

Game over. The hurdle posed by the abrogation of the two conflicting laws had been overcome, and Zimdar's worst nightmares soon became reality.

By seven o'clock that evening, the law was already in the official gazette. The public auction for the management of the electrical grid would soon be held, and interested companies had seven days to present their offer in a sealed envelope.

The news channels gave the extensive coverage of the story, including a public appearance by Mandeo, who wasted no time boasting of his victory.

The exhausted Zimdar left almost immediately, but not before informing Ariel that he would see him at seven o'clock the next morning.

Resigned to his fate by this time, Ariel returned home, and after a brief struggle to persuade his Razor to call Marianne, followed by another highly unsatisfying meal, he threw himself onto the bed without bothering to undress, bringing his first intense day of apprenticeship at the High Chamber of Populana to an end.

15. MEV

When Zimdar arrived punctually the next morning, Ariel was ready and waiting for him. Even though he detested the old man's morning routine, he had seen him so exhausted the day before that he had decided not to provoke him.

Not that he had actually planned to get out of bed when he had; he had woken up early as he often did when he had something important to do.

As soon as he saw how Zimdar was dressed, he knew they were going out somewhere.

"No voting today?" asked Ariel in surprise.

"Of course there is, but I have other things in mind for you, my young tyro. You have your license, I presume? I am too old to drive…"

"You bet!" smiled Ariel proudly. "Where are we going?"

"All in good time. First let us go to the garage for a car."

The cars designated for use by the High Representatives were regular electric cars like those used by the citizens of Populana.

It was not the frenzied building of Fusion Power Plants or the creation of an extensive distribution network that had allowed the country to abandon the use of fossil fuels once and for all.

The real revolution had been the MEV: cylindrical in shape, longer than it was wide, it was the size of a roll of kitchen paper, and slid into a housing on the hood of the car.

The MEV's strengths were its portability and simplicity of use: a single unit, fully charged, gave the automobile an autonomy of up to 550 miles, with a weight of just under four and a half pounds. The device took 24 hours to recharge fully, causing charging stations - where drivers could exchange their "flat" MEV for a fully-charged one - to sprout like mushrooms.

Despite its ease of use, few people outside those with a doctorate in physics would understand the precise workings of the cylinder, or how it was able to extract and store energy from that little vacuum cube on the inside.

Ariel was no different: his only knowledge of the MEV came from rumors and hearsay, such as the seemingly endless length of time taken by the MEV's inventor, Ganin Giar, to pay for all the damages caused during the early stages of its development before the foundation of Populana, when the battery had the nasty habit of emitting strong electromagnetic impulses which disabled all electronic equipment in the range of various miles. This catastrophic failure was to repeat itself a number of times, until its creator managed to develop a protective mechanism.

"Not bad!" thought Ariel, looking at the FT3-S he

had been assigned for that day. With its sporty lines, the car had a horsepower of 210, and he had heard some of his friends boasting of having driven it at 175 mph on the highway.

Sitting in the driver's seat, he hovered his identification code over the steering wheel, and was greeted by a seductive female voice. "Welcome Ariel Nat, you have traveled 20113 miles and committed 0 offences in the last 365 days. Your driving level is: expert. Urban speed limit: 30 mph. Extra-urban speed limit: 60 mph. Recommended speed on the highway: 90 mph.

"Where are we going?" Ariel asked the old man when the car had stopped talking.

"Chandaha," replied Zimdar.

"The Dead City? You're kidding, right?"

"Scared of ghosts, young tyro?".

"Not me," Ariel muttered, as he turned on the engine and drove out of the garage.

16. CHANDAHA

It was early, and the half-deserted streets allowed Ariel to put his foot down, to the delight of the powerful engine that purred in contentment.

"You're driving fast, young tyro, you must be very good," Zimdar observed once they were on the highway.

"Yup. What did you expect?", replied Ariel proudly

Populana's speed limits depended on the number of offences per mile committed by the driver in the last 365 days, a semi-assisted driving system deemed to be the right compromise ever since the safe co-existence between human beings and self-driving vehicles had proved to be somewhat of a utopia.

The protests of Brainzo, manufacturer of the Intellimobile, had fallen on deaf ears: people had absolutely no desire to behave like computers, and no program had been able to prevent people jaywalking or running red lights while cycling, which was probably why the Brainzo plant had been turned into a shopping mall after the Intellimobile had been banned.

"Do you have a theory about these sudden outages?" Zimdar asked abruptly.

"Not really," Ariel replied. "If the economy was doing well, I would have blamed the number of cars and higher energy demands from companies, but we're in the middle of a recession, so that seems unlikely. Plus, they've just built three new power stations, so it's all a bit puzzling."

"So?" Zimdar prodded.

"It's difficult to say, but surely it can't be a coincidence that Mandeo's proposal for the electrical grid has come up just when we're having these weird outages... Plus he's too smart to waste his only two laws on something that doesn't benefit him personally."

For the first time, there was an almost imperceptible smile of approval on the old man's lips.

"It sure is strange though," continued Ariel. "It certainly isn't Mandeo causing these outages, there's no way he could, but he might be exploiting them for his own ends."

"And what do you think those are?" asked Zimdar. "I'm sure he wasted no time bringing them up when he came to see you."

Ariel paused a moment before replying. "I don't know, to be honest I'm torn... My first instinct was that he was right..."

"Never lose sight of your honesty, young tyro", the old man murmured. "It is a precious gift."

They were so absorbed in conversation they hadn't noticed they were already at their destination.

Commonly known as the 'Dead City', Chandaha was a vast expanse of ruins at the southern border of the municipality of Allesia. Although centuries had passed since the Great War, none of Chandaha had been rebuilt, and had been left as a warning for the future generations.

Its large buildings were the semblance of a life that no longer existed, still bearing the heavy signs of the conflict. To protect them from the elements, every inch of the ruins had been painted using a transparent material, which also made them appear unnaturally shiny.

Although undoubtedly far from the founding fathers' intention, Chandaha had become a no-go area more than a memorial, and having been used as a location for various horror movies had only worsened its reputation.

Leaving the car in parking lot B of the mausoleum dedicated to the victims of the Great War, Ariel and Zimdar set out into the maze of streets of the ancient city.

17. LATROPP

"Looking for your house, Zim?" joked Ariel.

"I know I am an old ruin, but I am not *that* bad," Zimdar replied.

"Look," he went on, pointing to a gigantic billboard coated with the same material as the buildings.

Weather-beaten and punctured by a couple of bullet holes, an enormous face smiled out from the billboard, with the words 'VOTE Anton Latropp' above a round symbol consisting of a large 'V' and six small hexagons.

"What do you see?" asked Zimdar.

"A billboard asking people to vote for Anton Latropp, who I suppose is that clown with that stupid grin," Ariel replied.

"Anything odd about it?"

"Latropp's perfect skin, the impeccable hair, the white teeth, the makeup… and that symbol which I suppose is of his organization…".

"What's missing?" insisted Zimdar.

Ariel stared at the billboard for a moment before

replying resentfully: "What's missing are the answers to my questions."

"What questions?" the old man asked.

"First of all, why did you drag me all the way out here just to look at this idiot? It looks like an ad for a toothpaste, but the one I have suits me just fine, now that you guys have put me on a diet. And why would anyone vote for such a gormless idiot, anyway? For his smile? For his toupee? For that awful suntan? For the symbol? The poster sure doesn't say...."

"You are right," Zimdar nodded, "it does not say. On that billboard, the *image* of Anton Latropp had taken the place of *ideas*. With that advert, the only thing he was selling was himself."

"Well, it's understandable, I guess he had to pay his bills somehow. I bet that hairdo wasn't cheap!" Ariel joked.

"Exactly! And that brings us to our second point. Latropp was nothing but a tiny part of a more complex system. A campaign like that would have been extremely expensive. Who do you think financed it?"

"Whoever was able to..." Ariel replied, beginning to sense where the discussion was leading.

"Exactly. But why would anyone give money to a quack like Latropp?"

"Probably because there was something in it for them, since philanthropists are about as common as unicorns," Ariel replied.

"Agreed. So, would you believe me if I told you that Latropp's policies were not decided by his voters, but by those financing his campaign?".

"I guess so.... it would certainly ha for Latropp to betray strangers than tl his bills."

"And if I told you that Latropp stood as a candidate promising a redistribution of wealth, while being sponsored by rich multinational lobbies, what would you think?"

"I'd think that even if people were stupid enough to believe him, he sure wouldn't have been able to keep his promises."

"And that," Zimdar replied, "is exactly what happened. Latropp was leader of a movement that promised to transform the old political scene into one that benefitted the people. However, the movement was financed by big multinationals that had accumulated wealth at the expense of society, by funneling its revenues into countries that chose to look the other way. When he came to power, Latropp was forced to abandon his ideas to appease the powers that had supported him. The State, already heavily in debt, and unable to borrow from those who had bled it dry, increased taxation, and borrowed further funds from the very people who had robbed it in the first place. Over time, this policy exponentially widened the gap between rich and poor, until the economy was no longer able to support the parasites devouring it. To detract attention from his failures, Latropp and his sponsors laid the blame for the crisis on the populations of the bordering nations, who were going through similar hardship. They didn't have to work too hard to find the flimsy pretext that started the Great War, a conflict between the poorer classes that was supposed to lead to a redistribution of wealth, reducing the number of poor people without affecting the rich. But they miscalculated: the stockpiles of weapons were such that destruction was unthinkable. Not only did almost all of humankind perish, the war also wiped out the entire socio-economic system. Civilization was plunged into an era of darkness, that only came to an end when - years after the tragedy - a group of enlightened men decided to create a nation in the village we now know as Allesia. They built the first Tetron and adopted the system of choosing candidates at random from the population to prevent wealth from influencing the selection of its political representatives. The freedom we enjoy today, our democracy, is their legacy, and is all that separates us from barbarity."

The old man fell silent and the two continued walking through the streets of Chandaha.

The midday sun shone over the remains of the ancient city. Everywhere they looked, there were piles of rubble and desolation: little seemed to remain of the lives of those men who, despite everything, couldn't have been so different from those living in Allesia today.

"But what I'm wondering is… why Latropp? Why didn't they vote for someone else when they had the chance?" Ariel asked suddenly.

"Do you think it would have made any difference?" the old man asked. "The elections took place in a warped system - a race between a car and a bicycle. Only those who had the support of pre-existing powers could triumph, powers that demanded payment the day after the elections. Even if, by some miracle, things hadn't been that way, the nation's debt was in the hands of unscrupulous individuals, who could influence the political situation whenever they wanted. It was these aggregations of power and not the people who decided how politics should be. You see, that 24% of people who voted for Latropp…".

"24%?" interrupted Ariel, eyes wide in disbelief.

"Yes, 42% of the 57% with the right to vote. 24% of the electorate," replied Zimdar, before explaining. "The economy did not just suddenly collapse. There were premonitory signs - small crises and recessions. People started to suffer. It was clear as day that the concentration of wealth was killing the economy. As unrestrained as they were in their spending, a minority of wealthy citizens, certainly could not keep the economy afloat alone, and it was obvious it would soon collapse under the crushing weight of iniquity. Obviously, the politicians who preceded Latropp came from the same world he did. They certainly couldn't carry out a redistribution of wealth at the expense of those who were financing them, or worse, of those who were providing credit to the State. Instead of recognizing this limitation and working to change things, they laid the blame on a system of government that did not allow them to take effective decisions to pull the nation out of the recession. And so, they made sure of having a landslide victory in the event of a borderline electoral result. But they did not stop there: in their madness they even went as far as to subordinate legislative power to executive power. Unfortunately for them, they were the first victims of the economic crisis, and it was precisely the new system of government that allowed Latropp to trigger the series of events that almost brought civilization to an end."

"Sounds vaguely similar to Mandeo and all his talk about governability…" Ariel observed frowning.

Zimdar ignored his comment, almost as if to try to preserve that tiny flame of hope that was beginning to burn for Ariel. "Now, as I was saying, that 24% of the population who voted for Latropp were not guilty of choosing him over someone else. They were people like us who sincerely believed they were doing good. But it wasn't *who* they voted for that was the problem, but *how* they did it: they were convinced that anyone who voted otherwise was stupid, an idiot, weak, dishonest, a crook, a mobster, and so on and so forth. When the results came in, these same people, despite their claims of being democratic, believed 76% of their fellow citizens were people unworthy of contributing to the future of society. This was their biggest mistake - not realizing that freedom, equality and brotherhood, the founding principles of democracy, are bound by the invisible thread of faith in man. Every time we do not have faith in others, every time we feel we are better than them, every time that we feel we are irreplaceable, every time our truth makes us blind to the reasons of the next man… every time this happens, we hammer another nail into the coffin of democracy."

Ariel was silent for a moment: he felt as if he had received the answer to a question that had been plaguing him for some time, but one he couldn't quite put his finger on.

Pushing the thought aside with the promise to think about it later, he asked "But wasn't there anyone who said these things publicly? A journalist, maybe?"

"My young tyro," Zimdar replied gently, "journalists, just like everyone else, were having a field day in all of this mess. They were working for the government or for private publishers. If they'd tried to bite the hand that fed them, they'd have been out of work. Not even the narcissism of the most hardened columnists managed to shift the status quo one single centimeter. They were just a cog in the machine."

"But what about culture, education, showbusiness? Didn't anyone do anything?" he objected naively.

"Those were different times, Ariel," replied Zimdar, calling him by his name, something he never did. "Today, education and culture are the foundation of our society, and things could not be any other way, given that anyone can become a High Representative. Back then, however, there was not the slightest interest in instilling a sense of critical thinking in people: the risk they could come to doubt the fabulous promises of the candidates was just too great."

They walked on in silence for a few minutes until they came to a large ruined building.

"As far as showbusiness was concerned, take a look for yourself," murmured Zimdar, pointing to the remains of the great amphitheater.

Splashed across the only wing of the building left standing was an enormous banner with the words 'Tonight: Tafazz Sput on Tour! Time to stop! Vote Latropp!' The large 'V' of 'Vote' was in exactly the same style as the one he had seen previously on the billboard ad.

"Crikey!" Ariel exclaimed. "What the hell is this?"

"A lot of celebrities, including Tafazz Sput, used their popularity for political ends, and many political leaders went into showbusiness. During the final years, the lines began to blur, and it became very difficult to distinguish showbusiness from politics. Even some high-profile intellectuals made this mistake: anything is possible when style takes the place of substance."

"I see..." Ariel nodded, thinking that those crooks

would have had to come up with something to convince millions of people to vote for them when time was of the essence.

He stopped a moment to rest. All that talk was beginning to make him feel ill, and he was tired, almost exhausted, feeling the burden that had weighed on ordinary people like him just a few centuries before. Victims of a terrible economic crisis, unable to wrench the keys to the palace from the hands of those who were exploiting them.

Zimdar seemed to understand how he was feeling and relented. "Let us go on, young tyro, we have said more than enough for today. I simply wanted you to understand the events that brought you to that Chamber, and why you, Ariel Nat, an ordinary citizen, are so important for our democracy."

"You're right, old man," Ariel thought, "you've worn me out, although I've got to admit it's been pretty educational."

They wandered around the deserted city a little longer, pausing every so often to read some of the signs put up for tourists. 'Gas Station', 'Post Office', 'University', 'Supermarket'. The legacy of an ancient world mutilated by madness.

18. WAR

When the sun began to set, Zimdar wanted to head back, and Ariel didn't need to think twice, feeling that Chandaha was best avoided at night-time, and the two retraced their steps back to the remains of the great amphitheater.

Suddenly, Ariel stopped dead in his tracks. A slim figure was silhouetted against the darkening sky, near a big oak tree. Something was very familiar about that body...the shape, the height...the way it moved...

"Of course!" he thought. "It's the girl from the supermarket! What the hell is she doing *here*?"

Curious, he called out to her. "Hey!"

On hearing his yell, the girl turned and fled, and without a second thought, Ariel set off after her under Zimdar's incredulous gaze.

Ariel had never been particularly athletic, preferring to spend his free time sat in a VR chair playing videogames. But the first time he had made love to Marianne, he had realized she was a girl with standards, and so as not to disappoint her, he had begun working out regularly. It hadn't been easy, and he was certainly no ironman, but he'd built up a fair bit of stamina that now came in extremely handy.

When he got to the tree, he had almost caught up with her. Scrambling up a pile of rocks to his right, Ariel set off again after her, surrounded by majestic buildings that had once been teeming with life.

As he ran, he noticed a large armored tank in the middle of the street, its gun pointing left, its tracks picked apart by the passing centuries. It was right at that moment that the girl ducked into the door of an apartment block in the direction where the gun was pointing.

Seconds later Ariel caught up with her. The stairway was blocked by a pile of rubble: the girl was trapped and had nowhere to run.

They both stood there for a moment, breathing heavily, as if the same thief had stolen the breath from both their lungs, until she asked him "So why are you following me, *Mister* High Representative?"

"For the love of Zimdar," he said, taking a step towards her, "if you hadn't run off, you might have found out earlier."

"So, are you gonna explain what you're doing here?" the girl insisted, coming a little closer.

"I came for my groceries," he joked, sweat running rivers down his skin.

The girl raised her eyebrows for a moment, before her gaze returned to its neutral state.

"Sorry…" she said after a brief pause.

"For what?" he asked politely, thinking she meant the groceries.

"For *this!*" the girl fired back, kicking him hard in the private parts.

The pain was simply excruciating. A myriad of tiny flames tore through the darkness behind his eyelids, and a serpent of fire slid up through his bowels to the pit of his stomach, where it remained, slithering around his insides for the next five minutes, as Ariel writhed on the ground, unable to find a position that was any less painful.

Finally, Zimdar's voice cut through the haze. "Young tyro, you certainly have a way with women! I hope not all your relationships end this way," he joked as he helped him to his feet.

"Very funny old man, very funny," Ariel grunted as he got gingerly back on his feet.

"Let us go," his mentor said when Ariel had got his breath back, "enough games for today. It is time to go home."

19. FAITH

As they walked back to the car, Ariel couldn't stop thinking about the girl.

Who was she? Where did she live? What was she doing there? Why did every meeting with her end up going so wrong?

They got back to the car long before he resigned himself to the fact that the day was not going to bring the answers he had been looking for.

The return journey was very different: the dwindling light and the intensity of the day's events were taking their toll. Tired and in pain, Ariel drove slowly, thoughts whirling in his mind.

It wasn't just the mystery girl: Zimdar's words had unsettled him, and he was still having a hard time understanding how people like him could have caused so much suffering. The more he thought about it, the stranger he felt.

Suddenly he decided to break the long silence. "I keep asking myself why it was so difficult for people like us to believe in others, to the point of resorting to murder."

Zimdar drew a deep breath. "They were too absorbed in their own convictions to take any notice of those close to them. It does not matter how irrational it was: they would have believed in anything that could save them from having to acknowledge the unknown that underlies our very existence."

He went on: "You see, young tyro…when we are born, and we open our eyes to the universe for the first time, our mind is filled with the cosmic void that permeates it. Our natural instinct is to arrange that space to make it ours, defining what we call truth. There is no right or wrong way to do it; everyone follows their own path. Some choose religion, others superstition, or science, while others try to accept the void at the risk of losing themselves in it, given that the absence of truth is truth in itself. But that is not the point. The point is that all of us need some kind of truth, and when we finally create it, it risks driving us away from those who do not think the same way we do. Looking at the world through the eyes of others means realizing how little that illusion we have built is actually worth, and understanding that the reassuring room we have built is floating on an ocean of the unknown. Back then, people were prepared to do anything to prevent their little boat from sinking in that sea, even at the cost of killing their fellow men. They chose to die as prisoners in their own tiny house, instead of building a bigger one together with others."

"So how exactly were those people different from us?" Ariel interrupted him.

"In no way whatsoever. We are identical to them, the only difference being that we are still alive. Every day, we can still choose to break down the walls that we build around ourselves, in the knowledge that our lives are all intertwined. That is the only difference between a democratic faith and all the other religions that the human imagination has created ever since the dawn of time. The democrats choose to believe in the principles of freedom, equality and brotherhood, because believing in humanity is the only sensible choice for a man."

"A human being who doesn't believe in humanity is a bit of a contradiction in terms," Ariel agreed.

"Oh, my boy, you would be surprised how a religion that mortifies its followers can pave the way for an authoritarian government," Zimdar replied bitterly.

Ariel thought for a moment, unsure if the feeling of emptiness in his stomach was due to the kick, to hunger, or to those discussions that had unsettled him so much. "The unknown sure is scary", he said, "just the thought of not being fully in control of my own existence kind of freaks me out."

"My young tyro," Zimdar joked, "do not fret. If there was no such thing as chance, and your life was simply the result of a chain of cause and effect, you would have even less control than you do now. Maybe that is why you ended up with a fine fellow like me."

Their gazes crossed for a moment, and neither could contain their laughter. Ariel began to feel a real sense of affection for his gruff old mentor.

20. KAREN

"Oh, man…" thought Ariel, dismally surveying the mess he had managed to make in less than two days. Tomorrow he would call the cleaners to sort the place out.

But there was one positive note in all that chaos: the packet of cookies, sitting in that pile of crumbs he had left on the table, was the perfect antidote to his grumbling stomach.

He stuck his hand in the packet, but there were only a few left: that morning, before going to Chandaha, he'd almost finished the Zanco cookies.

As he brought the first one to his mouth, he was suddenly aware of an awful smell. "This thing stinks like a dead rat!" he said in disgust, then he realized it was his own hand he was smelling. Rolling around sweaty in the prehistoric dust of a dead city had its drawbacks.

Although he urgently needed a shower, he decided he would call Marianne first of all, tussling once more with the 'personal assistant no man should be with-out', cursing Charlie as he did so, despite the fact that old rivalry seemed little more than a distant memory.

But as her voice replaced the rhythmic rings of the telephone, he knew right away something was up.

"I'm worried," Marianne said. "It seems that Razor is about to lay off a whole bunch of people…"

"What, just like that?" Ariel asked, surprised.

"It's nothing official, just a rumor I heard from Karen Tanf, the vice-director. She and the director have gone over the books together and they're in the red: it seems that the drop in sales has been much worse than expected."

"Damn operating system, sometimes I think it was programmed by a moron!" Ariel muttered. "All that calculating power, wasted, really pisses me off!"

"Do you think it will affect us?" he asked, frowning, after a pause.

"No, sweetheart… Karen assured me your contract is protected by law, and that mine isn't at risk. At least someone at Razor appreciates what I do."

"And our colleagues?" he asked.

"I'm sorry, I don't know anything. Karen told me in confidence, she did it because we're friends, but she couldn't tell me anything else. Please don't say anything to anyone, or she might lose her job."

"Don't worry," he assured her.

"And how was your day?" asked Marianne.

"Different," Ariel replied. "Old Zimdar took me to Chandaha…"

"Chandaha? The Dead City?" she asked, incredulous.

"I had my doubts too, but he wouldn't listen to reason…" he laughed.

"I'm glad you're home safe and sound, sweetheart…"

"Oh, it's not so bad," he said, "the place has got a

bad rap, but it's practically deserted and there was hardly anyone around."

He stopped short in surprise.

Although not technically a lie, he couldn't understand why he had neglected to mention such an important detail. After all, he reasoned, there was no sense in talking about the girl before he knew the answers to the questions that his beloved Marianne would undoubtedly have asked him.

"How come the old man dragged you all the way out there?" Marianne asked, breaking the silence.

"I think he wanted me to understand why I've become a High Representative, and what my mission is…"

"And wouldn't the Chamber have been more appropriate?"

"No," replied Ariel thoughtfully. "I needed to see the world through the eyes of the people who chose this path for me."

"You're freaking me out!" she laughed. "You're starting to talk like some guru or other… I hope I don't find some old bearded guy in a robe in place of the carefree guy I fell in love with when this year's up!"

"Don't worry, there's no chance of that! You know how much I love all my little defects…"

The call ended affectionately amid their peals of laughter.

21. FANDAR

"I really need a good shower," thought Ariel, heading into the bathroom. But much to his annoyance, he had no sooner got undressed than he was forced to put his clothes back on. There was no hot water, and the thought of washing himself with the iced water spitting out of the taps made him shudder.

He brought the Razor to his lips and commanded: "Call the operator of the High Chamber."

"Good afternoon, this is Fandar Vul, how can I help Mr. Ariel Nat?" a polite voice asked, when the Razor finally deigned to collaborate.

"There's a problem with the hot water in my lodgings."

"I'm very sorry to hear that. Let me check which technician is available."

"Thank you so much!" replied Ariel, relieved.

After a short pause, the operator offered an embarrassed apology. "I am sorry, but unfortunately all Level One technicians are busy at the moment. Someone will be round tomorrow…"

"I'm just back from a long journey and I need to take a shower!" Ariel broke in, irritated. "I'm filthy! Do you expect me to sleep like some crocodile in a swamp?"

"I understand," Fandar replied. "Let me send old Joe Plum, who helps out when we are short-staffed. Do not worry, although he is not Level One accredited, he is good and reliable. Afterwards I will send a technician to ensure everything has been done properly. Just a formality."

"Thank you," Ariel replied. "I appreciate it."

"Not at all. Let us know if you need anything else," the operator replied and hung up.

22. JOE

Joe Plum arrived punctually half an hour later. Short and sturdy, dressed in an old-fashioned pair of dungarees, he filled the entire width of the doorway. The muscles of his youth had softened with age, but his arms were still well-toned and covered with soft white hair, the suspenders and backpack with his tools on one shoulder completing the rather comic picture of an overgrown schoolboy you couldn't help but like.

"Hey kid," Joe greeted him without hesitation. "They told me you've got a problem of some sort."

"I think I may have more than one," replied Ariel with a grin, "but the one you're looking for is that way."

Amused, the old man followed him to the bathroom.

Ariel turned on the tap. "As you might have noticed when you came in, I stink like a pig that's been rolling around in the mud, but if I have a shower with the ice that's coming out of here, I may well end up in the frozen foods department."

"Oh, I've smelled much worse in my time, believe me," the handyman smiled, running his hand under the water. "You're right, it *is* cold. Must be the safety valve. These valves are designed to close when there's no power. Normally the power's always on and the valves stay open for a long time, but the recent outages have put this old system under stress, and the technicians have been submerged with calls. That's why they dragged me out of bed this morning."

"Can you fix it?" asked Ariel anxiously.

"Sure can. I've got a couple of new-generation valves here. As a precaution, I'll also replace the cold-water valve, because normally they break around the same time."

The old man set his backpack down beside the hydraulic panel and took out two valves, a screwdriver, a pair of adjustable pliers, a can of spray lubricant, a mat and a mini vacuum cleaner.

He placed the mat under the panel, opened it with the screwdriver, and thoroughly vacuumed the hydraulic box, that clearly hadn't seen the light of day in a very long time.

When he had finished, he closed the two taps upstream of the valves, removed the connectors, and sprayed lubricant into the gaps on either side of the fixing nuts. He then removed the old valves, using the pliers to loosen them from years of disuse.

A little water ran on to the mat as the old man removed a metal object from its housing. "See here, this is the jammed valve," he explained with an air of satisfaction.

Ariel watched Joe with a certain admiration, and the handyman, after having installed the new valves, repeated the entire process in reverse.

"You're really good, it's a pleasure to watch you work!" Ariel complimented him, as he ran his fingers under the jet of hot water spilling from the tap.

"Let's just say I was lucky. These old valves might have snapped, and then you'd have seen me sweat! My dad always said it's not the lack of errors that makes a good craftsman, but how you solve them."

"Your dad was right!" Ariel said approvingly, "computer programming is exactly the same!"

"Oh wow... a programmer! I haven't met one since I worked at Modelbyte!" Joe exclaimed.

"You worked at Modelbyte?" asked Ariel, incredulous.

"Yup." The old man sighed. "But it was a long time ago."

"Would you like a cup of tea?" Ariel asked. "It's good to meet a colleague every once in a while."

"But what about your shower?"

"I've waited this long, five minutes more won't kill me. Besides, you said you've smelt much worse before today, so I've given up worrying about your nose."

Joe smiled and sat down, while Ariel set about making the tea. "Can I ask how a Modelbyte technician ended up as a plumber at the High Chamber of Populana?"

Joe let out another sigh, but did not reply. "Sorry," Ariel said, "that was inappropriate. I was just curious; you don't have to answer if you don't want to."

"Don't worry kid, I didn't get to this age so I could pretend to be someone I'm not. It was the betting that did it. I was hooked on gambling."

"Did you lose all your money on the Intelliraces?"

"Some of it. But not just there. I bet on everything, from the tiniest things to the most important, like my job. And sadly, I lost that one."

"I'm sorry," Ariel murmured as he poured the tea.

"Don't be sorry. I wouldn't have done it if I hadn't wanted to. Lucky for me, after being knocked down time and time again, life taught me that the only bet you're sure to win is the one you never make. I swore I'd never gamble again, and I've been clean ever since."

"What was it like working at Modelbyte?" Ariel asked to lighten the atmosphere.

"It was my life. The Modelbyte robots are at the cutting edge, perhaps the most advanced systems ever conceived by human intelligence. And if you think that the Modelbytes used to build houses are infinitely simpler than those used for the Tetrons, you can understand how exciting it was."

Ariel nodded. "To be honest, I'm intrigued by the mystery of the Modelbyte robots that stay inside the Fourth Room of the Tetrons. It's been my obsession ever since I was young, and I've spent many nights awake, wondering what might be inside."

"I know what you mean, shame there's no way of knowing" Joe gazed at him in sympathy.

"You must have come to some conclusion working for Modelbyte…".

"The only thing we know," the old man said, "is that whatever's in there, the Tetron network is the memory of our civilization. All our systems interface with this distributed intelligence that knows everything about us: our name, our identification number, our biometric data, our belongings, our criminal record, and so on and so forth. Our lives, from the cradle to the grave, happen in the Tetrons."

"But this is all pretty much common knowledge!" Ariel broke in. "I work for Razor and I interface with the Tetrons every day to identify the users and for the transactions…"

"You're right," Joe smiled, "but if you think about it, this network seems to go beyond the capabilities of the Modelbyte robots, which, as far as I know, are the only form of intelligence installed in a Tetron at the time of construction."

Old Joe was right. As powerful as they were, the individual Modelbyte robots could not explain the mysterious functioning of that network, or its ability to adapt to the needs of a society that was constantly changing.

"So the answer must lie in what's built inside the Fourth Room," Ariel said, pondering.

"Maybe, but the only way to find out would be to become an ectoplasm and slip through the walls. That would be the only way to find out what those damned robots do."

Ariel drowned his dissatisfaction in a mouthful of tea before continuing. "Whatever's in there must need a lot of power to do all that work. I wonder if these outages might become a problem for the Tetrons, seeing as they're powered by electricity."

"Not for the first six days, I don't think," the old man said thoughtfully. "Not that I have any actual data to back it up, but that's the operating autonomy of the MEV powering the Modelbyte that stays in each pyramid. As far as I know, there's no other equipment in the Fourth Room that's connected to the grid."

"What do you make of these outages?" Ariel interrupted him.

Joe gazed at him for a moment before he spoke. "I

was talking about this the other day with a technician from the electrical company who was at his wit's end about the power cuts. He asked my opinion, showed me some figures. The power surges are happening all over the country. The last three outages happened at 1:15 on Tuesday, 2:56 on Thursday and 4:40 on Friday. The power consumption in the residential areas and in the Tetrons has spiked for one or two seconds on various occasions, but no-one knows why. Now, if the increase was gradual, the grid would be able to compensate without any problem, but such sudden surges are impossible to manage, since keeping production at a maximum for the whole day would be incredibly wasteful."

"Your memory is amazing!" observed Ariel in admiration. "How do you just reel off those dates like that? I have trouble remembering how old I am sometimes!"

"I have a photographic memory and remember everything I see…"

"Lucky you!"

"I would be if I could choose what to remember," said Joe with a bitter smile, "but my mind loves to torture me with the worst images it can dredge up. I suppose that's why I try to keep it busy."

"Going back to what we were saying," Ariel said, frowning, "the pattern of these outages is awfully suspicious. It's almost like they're causing them deliberately."

"Watch it, kid," Joe warned him. "You may be right, but you're on very thin ice. For safety's sake, there are things I keep to myself."

But Ariel couldn't stop thinking about the three outages. "1:15 on Tuesday, 2:56 on Thursday, 4:40 on

Friday, all in the afternoon. Let's see, we're looking for some device that can increase power consumption, both in people's homes and in the Tetrons... something connected to the grid..."

"Wait!" he exclaimed, clapping his hand to the back of his neck.

"Of course! 2:56... I know that time! It was when I had the accident on the Kurmar VR chair, and the technicians talked about a power surge... of course.... it must be the chairs that are causing these outages!"

Joe stared at him open-mouthed: not only had that kid, who if truth be told seemed a bit of a halfwit, arrived at the same conclusions he had, but even had proof of the Kurmar VR chair's guilt tattooed on his skin.

The old handyman's expression darkened, and worry crept into his eyes. He was silent for a while, but when he spoke, his voice was sharp. "You're a smart kid, so I'm only gonna say this once. Even if what you say is true, you've no proof to back up your accusation. I mean it, you need to be careful. The world's changed: today corporations like Kurmar Enterprise have a power that people could only dream about just decades ago, and what you've discovered proves it. If they knew they couldn't get away with it, they wouldn't even try."

"I should go," he added, swinging his backpack on to his shoulder. "If you know what's good for you, you won't mention this to anyone. Good luck, kid," said Joe as he walked out of the door.

23. DOUBT

Ariel was too agitated to sleep.

The Kurmar VR chairs, the electricity surges, the outages, the bill proposed by Mandeo… everything was connected, he was sure of it. But why?

Even if Kurmar succeeded in gaining ownership of the electrical company, what advantage could this possibly have in a world so interconnected with the Tetrons?

Turning them off would be tantamount to suicide, given that the very structure of society and all its data were saved in their memories. Without the Tetrons, Kurmar's entire network of power would dissolve.

"No, it's impossible…" thought Ariel, turning over in bed. "There's still something I'm missing."

But it was not only this realization that kept him awake. Joe's warning still rang in his ears.

"Am I in danger? Who can I trust? No, not Marianne, she wouldn't understand… and not my parents either, I can just see my dad on the phone to the shrink right now…"

He had no choice. Zimdar was the only person whose loyalty to Populana was unequivocal.

But one doubt remained: would the old man be able to control himself, or would he drag him into a holy war, sacrificing his life on the altar of truth?

There was nothing for it.

For the first time in his life, Ariel felt the need for advice and guidance.

24. LIGHT

The following morning, Zimdar arrived as punctual as ever, but for once it did not bother the anxious Ariel.

"My young tyro, this girl has really got the better of you," his mentor said, looking at him in concern. "It looks like you have been run over by a juggernaut. Let me buy you breakfast."

"Not today," Ariel interrupted him. "I have to talk to you in private. Come in."

"Very well. I will be back in a moment," the old man replied. Noticing the worry on Ariel's face, he left him alone for a few minutes, coming back armed with pastries and a quart of milk.

"You should at least eat some breakfast," Zimdar said, setting the food on the table.

"Thanks," said Ariel, grabbing a pastry. "There's something I need to tell you."

"Go on."

"Yesterday, while I was talking to Joe Plum from the maintenance service, I realized that these outages might be the work of Kurmar Enterprise."

"That is a very serious accusation. What makes you think that?" the old man asked in surprise.

"The suspicious power surges come from the residential areas and from the Tetrons, both of which have VR chairs. Plus, this mark on my neck was caused by an energy surge at the same time as the outage at 2:56 on Thursday, right when I was sitting in the chair in the great pyramid in Novardia."

Zimdar knitted his eyebrows in one of the typical expressions he always made when his thoughts went off on a tangent.

After a very long pause, the old man seemed to gather his thoughts and nodded. "I see. Why do you think they are doing it?"

"I don't know, but I don't think they want to deactivate the Tetrons, because their power is dependent on them."

The old man agreed. "You are right: the point here is not destruction, but control."

"But there's something I don't understand," Ariel said. "What control would they have over the Tetrons by messing with the electricity network? It's a complex system, not like a light bulb you can just turn on and off… Unless…"

"Unless?" the old man echoed curiously.

"Why didn't I think of it before?" exclaimed Ariel, clapping his hand to his forehead. "Even a light bulb that flashes on and off can be used to communicate. Like everyone, I always believed that the Tetrons communicated with each other exclusively by air. But they're also all connected to the same electrical grid, and if they modulated a signal on that network, that would explain why no-one has ever managed to fully understand how they work: they were missing one very important piece of the puzzle! And that would also explain Kurmar's interest in taking control of the electrical company."

Zimdar remained lost in thought for a little. "I think you have hit the nail on the head, young tyro. The matter is more serious than I thought: if Kurmar managed to gain control of the Tetron network, it would have absolute power over society, the dream of all the worst dictators in history. We will end up living just like our ancestors, slaves to the illusion of being free."

"So, what do we do?"

"Nothing for the moment," the old man replied. "To catch a snake, you must wait until it ventures out of its burrow. If we act too soon, they will go back to scheming in the shadows, only to strike us when we least expect it. We must be patient and not waste our advantage. We shall wait for the results of the auction to see if our suspicions are founded. It is only a few days away."

"Alright, let's keep it to ourselves until the time's right," said Ariel approvingly, before biting into the last pastry.

25. KARMA

The days that followed were uneventful, with nothing to disturb their routine as High Representatives.

Ariel got to know some of the people who had received the Call just as he had. An eclectic sample of humanity: some very active, some lazy, some selfish, some generous, some apathetic, some committed, some open, some obtuse... ordinary men and women, each with their own idea of what politics should be. Some felt honored to be part of that group, others saw it as an unpleasant intrusion, others still as a mission. Their intentions, too, were just as varied: some tried to do good, others to turn it to their advantage: others - luckily not many - showed that gratuitous malice that Zimdar described as the first sign of stupidity.

"If you really have to do wrong," he said, "at least do it with some sort of purpose, because that wrongdoing is going to come back to haunt you, and if you do not have some kind of a goal, you will be left with nothing."

It all had to do with his idea of existence founded on the principle of action and reaction. "You see, my young tyro," his mentor would say, "our way of acting profoundly influences the environment in which we live, through the feedback of those around us. This means that reality often responds to us, depending on how we relate to it. For example, if you go into a room and start shooting, you might get away with it once, but you should expect to be shot at some day or other. In the same way, if you steal from others, do not be surprised if you find yourself deprived of your money or your freedom." Or "if you lie to live, you will live to lie. If you seize power by force, then do not expect to be able to govern without it. He who lives by the sword, dies by the sword." Or even "if a woman leaves someone else to be with you, she might do the very same to you one day." Or finally "if you treat people badly, do not expect them to treat you well."

Ariel found he actually enjoyed listening to the old man's pearls of wisdom, and he seemed to have one for every occasion.

Between the various sessions and sermons, Ariel even had some time to phone his family and to call Marianne.

Things with her were not going well.

Although his political adventure had only just begun, the distance between them was already leaving its mark. His intriguing investigations had finally given Ariel the perspective he had been looking for, and now he had found it, he wasn't about to let it go.

Marianne reacted to this change with suspicion, and grew impatient at his unusual enthusiasm for politics. Often they struggled to find the right topics of conversation, and communicating with her became more and more frustrating.

But his troubles with Marianne were not the only thing bothering him. The stranger who had got the better of him twice had wormed her way firmly into his thoughts.

One day as he was leaving his lodgings, he thought he saw her hurrying into one of the elevators, but his hopes were dashed when the doors closed before he could get to her.

He found an excuse to wander through the aisles of the supermarket on a number of occasions, but all in vain. She seemed to have disappeared into thin air, and Ariel began to resign himself to the idea that he would never discover her identity.

26. SURPRISE

The day the auction results were announced was the first day of Ariel's second week, and from that moment on, it would be him who had to speak and vote in the Chamber.

Zimdar's time as a High Representative was almost at an end. He would act as Ariel's adviser for the rest of that week, before going back to his own life once and for all: he was more likely to be hit by a meteorite than be selected for a third time.

Ariel looked around him, his excitement growing. The High Representatives were all settling down in their places, while the moderator waited for the results he would be announcing to appear on the screen. Mandeo was beaming: just a few minutes more, and he would be closer than ever to seeing his dream come true.

The moderator tapped three times on the microphone and waited for silence before he spoke. "Colleagues, the official results of the auction will now appear on your monitors…"

Both Mandeo and Ariel felt the same shiver run down their back as the moderator announced: "Six offers have been received.

Zarco Limited: 30.790.000 schlepps
Novalit United: 35.900.000 schlepps
Dapos Limited: 37.300.000 schlepps
Vagrand Extended: 45.850.000 schlepps
Kurmar Enterprise: 400.000.000 schlepps
Razor Corporation: 500.000.000 schlepps

I therefore announce the Razor Corporation as the winner of the auction, subject to verification of availability of the necessary funds, as prescribed by law. The Chamber is adjourned until 2 pm."

A ripple of voices ran through the Chamber. The auction had been a success. 500 million schlepps was an enormous sum.

Ariel, who had not taken his eyes off Mandeo for a moment, saw his triumphant expression twist into a fleeting grimace of surprise, before his usual poker face slipped back into place.

Zimdar noticed it too. "Strange reaction for someone who has just managed to earn the State such an enormous sum…" he murmured.

Ariel was sure his previous hunch had not been wrong. Mandeo probably expected someone else to win the auction. Something had gone wrong.

But what?

He opened his mouth to speak, but the old man gave an almost imperceptible shake of his head. "Better to talk about this in the privacy of your lodgings. Come, there is nothing more to see here."

27. RAZOR

Back in his apartment, Ariel could no longer contain his amazement. "This is really weird! Let's see if we can make some sense out of this mess."

"Go on," Zimdar encouraged him, after making sure the door was firmly closed behind them.

"So," Ariel opened with a flourish, "we have reason to believe that Kurmar Enterprise caused these outages to give greater weight to Mandeo's proposal. The laws in question, the only two proposed by our friend, have been approved, to his immense satisfaction. He's invested everything in those two babies, and given his requests for support, I'm convinced he's trying to bring in a different method of selecting the High Representatives, something that would only be possible by cutting the electricity supply to the Tetrons. In fact, it wouldn't possible to introduce the role of professional politician without deactivating the current selection system. However, we have reason to think that Mandeo's ambition has exceeded his intelligence on this occasion, given that shutting down the

Tetrons would have thrown the country into a state of chaos with risks much too big for the those responsible. Kurmar, on the other hand, according to our theory, was aiming to control the system by analyzing the flow of data that's secretly running through the electrical grid. That would have guaranteed it almost complete power without anyone noticing. This interest is confirmed by their enormous offer, that would almost certainly have won them the auction, if the Razor Corporation hadn't made one that was even crazier."

"What do you know about Razor? I know you work there," Zimdar interrupted him.

"Only what everyone else knows."

"You know I am not very technologically-minded," the old man apologized with a touch of shame.

"You don't say..." Ariel said with a sly grin. "Well, the Razor Corporation was founded fifteen years ago, when the Larvini brothers designed a program that was able to accumulate an immense quantity of data in very little time. As you know, the information in the big networks is arranged in cards. To display one, you just enter its address in an application called a browser. The first part of this path is called a domain, and it identifies the set of cards it refers to. Vongol, the browser designed by the Larvini brothers, was identical to the others in almost every way, but with two major differences. First of all, it had been designed to transmit the cards displayed to the central server, allowing it to store all their contents. Then - and this was what made it so successful - it paid up to 10,000 schlepps per day to anyone who manually visited a domain that wasn't yet indexed by the Razor…".

"It must have cost them a fortune!" remarked Zimdar, incredulous.

"Not exactly… the amount paid for each new addition was inversely proportional to the number of domains already registered in the server. To put it simply, the first 9 new domains displayed using Vongol earned users the considerable sum of 10.000 schlepps each. The subsequent uploads from the 10th to the 99th earned users a thousand schlepps, the 100th to the 999th a hundred… from the 1000th to the 9999th ten, and so on, decreasing as the uploads increased. The obsessive advertising campaign and easy earnings in the initial stages drew an immense number of greedy users, dazzled by the promise of making money simply by browsing the Great Network. The number of domains in the Razor's index grew exponentially, so much so that after only a few days, a new upload was worth just thousandths of schlepps, before becoming millionths and even billionths. Soon people were no longer earning anything at all, but they continued to use Razor's services, since they'd got accustomed to using Vongol as the default browser, and its search engine as the only way to find information online."

"That program must have worked very well to be so successful," remarked the old man in admiration.

"Absolutely not," Ariel replied. "Razor didn't win for its quality. Vongol was pretty crap, its search function too, that was missing a lot of information compared to its competitors. But it swept them away thanks to the monstrous amount of information it managed to accumulate in an extremely short space of time, thanks to the illusion of making a quick buck.

By this time, not only did it have the most complete index of all the cards in the network, it could also study the behavior of its users in detail, since they had entered their personal information into the browser to receive payments. It didn't take Razor long to realize that having a monopoly over network searches was like sitting on a gold mine. Controlling the order that the results were displayed, and generally controlling access to information allowed them to sell the privilege of appearing first. The advertising made them tons of money that they decided to re-invest by creating a personal assistant that was the portable version of Vongol, and they called it Razor after the company," he concluded, indicating the screen he carried on his forearm.

Zimdar nodded and remained in silence for a moment, as if digesting all that information. Then he said: "I think I read something about Vongol some time ago, but I thought it was a fishing company."

"You're right," Ariel smiled. "Unfortunately for the Larvini brothers, the High Chamber of Populana ordered the closure of Vongol four years ago with the law (0342-16) on the neutrality of the Great Network, deeming it inadmissible that a private company could influence access to online information using such murky practices. Vongol's card index was confiscated, and searches are now managed according to a neutral algorithm by the GNPB, the Great Network Public Body. Since then, all that's left of Razor is this device," he explained, touching his arm, "and just between you and me, I know from a reliable source that sales have taken a nosedive, and they'll soon be laying people off because of a lack of money…"

"Are you quite sure?" Zimdar objected, his brows

furrowed. "That does not sound very credible, considering they have just offered five hundred million schlepps for the electrical company."

"That *is* strange, come to think about it," conceded Ariel, his gaze darkening.

"Something does not add up," Zimdar said. "Let us consult the Razor Corporation's financial statements. The information is in the public domain. Get your tablet."

"Eh? What tablet?"

"I thought you were smarter than that, my boy," the old man teased, talking a palm-sized device from what looked like a picture hanging on the wall. "Every High Representative has one. And this is yours."

"And how am I supposed to know if no-one tells me?" Ariel protested.

Zimdar smiled, savoring the moment. "You are right. But I never use mine. When I got somewhat paranoid during my first mandate, I would go down to the data room and get a printout on paper. Then I stopped looking at the financial statements and resigned myself to trusting the data, like everyone else. The Tetron system, after all, never fails."

Holding out the tablet, he added "You do it, I am not very good with these things."

Ariel brought up the GNPB search engine, and gave a command in a loud, clear voice. "Company information and financial statements for the Razor Corporation."

A moment later, the data appeared beautifully ordered on the screen, as a female voice announced "Here is the company information and financial statements for the Razor Corporation, registered in the name of Cei and Cli Larvini. Is this what you were looking for?"

"Look at this!" exclaimed Ariel. "According to this, Razor has more than a billion schlepps in cash assets, and has been in the black to the tune of 300 million schlepps over the last trimester. I wonder if Karen, the vice-director of Razor who gave my girl-friend the information, was smoking something weird when she was looking at the books."

"It is all very strange," nodded Zimdar. "But the data does not lie, and it would not be the first time that a company claims to be sinking so it can squeeze a little more out of its workers...".

"To the point of spreading fake rumors to close friends?" Ariel asked irritably.

"It is a little bizarre," the old man admitted, "but that is not the point."

"So, what *is* the point?" Ariel snapped.

"My young tyro, I understand that you work for this company and that you feel involved, but there is something much bigger than us at stake here, and we must not lose our heads. The point is that Razor pipped Kurmar to the post with an extremely large offer, one that is difficult to justify given the safe-guards the law has put in place to prevent companies making a profit from users of essential services. They will never manage to recover from this absurd in-vestment before the concession expires."

"I'm sorry, you're right. So now we have double trouble, seeing as there are now two suspects. Do you think the bidders are in it together?"

"Perhaps, but it seems improbable. If they were, Kurmar would not even have taken part in the auc-tion to protect itself from those who, like us, might have guessed its involvement in the outages. I am not sure, but I think that in this case, there are two wolves contending the same prey."

"I've got an idea…" Ariel said, before consulting the GNPB search engine. "Company information and financial statements for Kurmar Enterprise."

The kind voice on the device announced "Here is the company information and financial statements for Kurmar Enterprise, registered in the name of Patron Naltop. Is this what you were looking for?"

"I think you're right about the two wolves," Ariel said, pointing at the screen. "Kurmar has a liquidity of 492.936.442 schlepps. By offering five hundred million, Razor knew it could beat Kurmar, even if the company used practically all its assets…"

"It may be a clue, but it is hardly conclusive," objected Zimdar, skeptical.

Ariel scratched his arm nervously. "It's true, you're right, it doesn't prove anything, but it seems awfully weird that both of them would make such stratospheric offers away from the market for no good reason. Though if our theory is correct, and Razor's offer *was* made against Kurmar, it means there's been a leak somewhere. I wonder how Razor knew about the interest of its rivals…"

"I do not know, young tyro, but if *we* guessed their intentions, maybe Razor did too… or maybe someone talked, although I do not know who. There are too many "ifs" in our theory for my liking, and we risk losing our way.

"It is getting late," said the old man. "There will be a new session soon and we had better not draw attention to ourselves. Let us sleep on it, and come back to it tomorrow with a clear head."

28. ABYSS

They met later in the Chamber, but Ariel's head was elsewhere, all his brain cells focused on trying to understand Karen's strange behavior, and how Razor could have found out what Kurmar was playing at.

What followed was almost comical: first Ariel sat in the wrong seat, then he called Zimdar "Marianne" a couple of times, before being given an official warning from the moderator when his Razor rang at the most inappropriate moment in the session.

There was nothing for it, multitasking really wasn't his thing, and both he and Zimdar were extremely relieved when they finally got back to their respective lodgings.

Worried about the unusual time that Marianne had phoned, Ariel called her the minute he got in.

When she replied, Marianne was livid. "Who did you tell?" she demanded.

"What, sweetheart?"

"Don't pretend you don't know! What Karen confided to me about the layoffs!"

"No-one, of course!" he objected, omitting to tell her about his earlier conversation.

"Don't lie to me! You know she was fired this morning?"

"That's awful! I'm so sorry, but it's got nothing to do with me... maybe someone overheard you talking?"

"Impossible! She told me when we were having dinner at our house and there was no-one else with us!"

"I honestly don't know what to say, but it's all very weird: you told me Karen said Razor was in the red, but they've just invested five hundred million schlepps to acquire the electrical company. I've looked at their books and they've got over a billion in liquidity... Something's not right, but don't you worry, I'm gonna find out what's..."

"I don't know who you are anymore!" Her voice rose to a shriek. "Don't you see you're throwing away everything we ever had?"

"But hon, it's my job!"

"See, that's *exactly* what I'm talking about! Your job and your life are here with me at Razor, not in that freaking hospice! That damn mentor of yours has poisoned your mind!"

"Don't talk about the venerable old man like that! I'm the only one who can insult him!" joked Ariel to ease the tension.

Marianne did not laugh. She gave a long sigh, and when she spoke, her voice was filled with an immense sadness. "I need this job. Ariel, I don't think this is going to work. You and I have chosen different paths. You're not the guy I fell in love with, and it's obvious you don't care about me anymore. I've thought about us a lot over the last few days. If you want to throw your life away, fine. But don't take me with you. I think we need some time apart."

There was silence for what seemed like an eternity: neither of them seemed to have the words to fill the abyss that had opened between them. Finally, it was Marianne who whispered simply "I'm sorry...". And she hung up.

Ariel threw a tremendous punch at the wall, before throwing himself disconsolately on to the bed. He desperately wanted to cry, but no tears came. He felt empty, and if he'd had the strength, he would have torn open his chest to see if it still held a beating heart.

29. SARA

He lay there lifeless for a couple of hours, until an insistent ringing pulled him back to reality.

It took a few seconds to realize it had to be the door, and eventually he dragged himself up unwillingly to see who was making all that noise. After all, whatever was behind those walls certainly couldn't make his day any worse. Not only had Marianne left him, but if he went on like this, he'd probably lose his job too.

But to his immense surprise, on opening the door, he found himself face to face with the mystery girl.

As soon as he saw her, Ariel shook his head, resentment hardening his reply. "No way! Look, just go. This is really not a good time - I've had my share of kicks in the balls for one day!"

He moved to close the door, but she pushed past him and darted inside. "You've got to let me in, or I'm done for!"

"Hey! What the... well this is just great! Now there's a freaking psychopath in my house!" thought

Ariel, shutting the door. "And there was me thinking things couldn't get any worse..."

But when he turned around, the figure he saw was a far cry from that assured, feisty figure who had sent him crashing to the ground twice: fragile and terror-stricken, beads of sweat stood out on her forehead, her gaze darting nervously around the room in search of somewhere safe.

"I hope you've got a good reason for gatecrashing my apartment like this," Ariel said curtly.

The girl was silent, not having had time to think up a credible excuse for bursting in.

"What kind of awful person must I be that no-one's prepared to trust me one little bit," thought Ariel bitterly.

Suddenly, he could no longer contain his anger. "Listen, my day so far has been shitty to say the least. All I've had from you so far is bruises... I didn't ask you to come here! So now, either you trust me and you tell me the truth, or you can get the hell out... I'm not kidding!"

The girl gazed at him in astonishment for a few moments, and when she spoke, her voice was barely audible. "Okay. I guess I don't have a choice..."

"What did you say?" Ariel said sharply.

"Ssssh, keep your voice down!" she urged him. "I'll tell you everything, I promise, but please don't shout. They're looking for me and if they find me, I'm done for!"

"Let's sit down there," she offered, sitting down and huddling into the furthest corner of the room. "I don't want anyone to hear us."

Ariel obliged her strange request, sitting down next to her on the cold floor.

She sat for a few minutes, her head bowed, then she spoke. "I don't know where to start, so I'll get straight to the point. I've been working here as a Level One cleaner for three months. Every day I clean the lodgings of eight High Representatives. It's not a great job, but it pays well. But that's not why I do it. I didn't go to university just to become a cleaner..."

"So why *do* you do it?" interrupted Ariel curiously.

"Bear with me, I'll get to that in a minute... my parents died when I was young, and my grandpa Karl has always been the world to me. He always gave me everything I needed, everything I wanted, and I never took too much notice of what happened to other people... But one day, four years and one week ago, knowing he didn't have much time left, my grandpa took me to Chandaha, and in the shadow of that big oak tree near the amphitheater, he told me a story that goes back to the time of the foundation..."

"Just as well she wanted to get straight to the point..." thought Ariel, in a feeble attempt to rekindle his rage that was fast slipping away in the face of her gentleness and embarrassment.

The girl turned to scrutinize him for a moment, as if searching for some kind of pretext to clam up once more, but found none. All of Ariel's aggression and anger had drained away, replaced by a mixture of tenderness and curiosity.

A tiny shiver ran through her, and she looked towards the floor, gazing into space.

"Do you want to stop?" Ariel asked her gently.

She replied: "No, it's just that... I've never told anyone these things... you're the first, but it's the only way I can make sense of everything... and after everything that's happened, I owe it to you."

With great effort, the girl began telling the story of her grandfather. "The Great War was over by this time. The world was destroyed. Civilization was mortally wounded. Of what was once the charming town of Chandaha, there was nothing left but rubble and desolation. The few remaining survivors, a hundred or so young reserves, unaware of the destruction of their headquarters, fought in the streets of the deserted city. They had been ordered to resist at all costs, and to wait for backup that would never arrive. The fighting raged violently for several weeks, and the numbers continued to dwindle until only a dozen or so soldiers were left on each side. They were all on their last legs: supplies had long since dried up, and they were surviving on nothing but insects and stray cats and dogs. One day, the Marvans, who still had an armored tank, finally managed to corner the Kurzi in the atrium of a building. Exhausted and without ammunition, they had nowhere to run… the gun was pointed in their direction, everything was ready. A single shot, and victory was theirs. Roger Mann, commander of the Marvans, gave the order to shoot, but when Geoa Stark, the weapons officer, fired, the shell jammed in the chamber. At that point, Roger completely lost his mind. He exploded out of the tank like an atomic bomb, he started shaking the gun, screaming at the top of his voice, a torrent of words that made no sense, pouring all the rage he had accumulated during those years of senseless massacre on to that huge hunk of metal. Then all of a sudden, Tara Tric, the commander of the Kurzi, crept out of her hiding place. The tank crew couldn't shoot her because their superior was in the line of fire. They tried to signal to Roger that the enemy was approaching, but he was so wrapped up in his own fury that he was oblivious to everything and everyone. Then Tara was right behind him, but instead of killing him, she came up beside him and started hitting and insulting the tank as well. If it hadn't been so tragic, that picture would have been funny: a man and a woman trying to destroy an armored vehicle with their words and their fists. At any other time, two people like that would have been hustled off to a mental institution. Instead, first one, then two, then four, then eight, then sixteen… all the soldiers from both sides came to join them, and the streets of Chandaha were echoing with that strange music of percussion and imprecations for a long time afterwards. That crazed and random gesture brought more peace than guns ever could. That same night, that group of men and women came together around the fire, voting unanimously to bury their uniforms and destroy their weapons, deciding that war would no longer have a place in their lives. They decided that they would work together to build a new civilization, and that to prevent conflict between the old factions, the roles of each would be decided by way of a draw. They gave themselves new names, and made a blood pact, swearing on their own lives that they would dedicate all their energies to rebuilding society, based on the principles of freedom, equality and brotherhood, so that no-one would ever have to go through a similar tragedy. That was the dawn of the world we're living in now."

"That's not the version they teach at school," Ariel thought, when she finished speaking. "I bet not even Zimdar knows anything about it, otherwise the sight of that armored tank would have sent him into fury."

"Incredible," he admitted, gazing warmly at the

young woman. "I've never heard this version of events."

"If what my grandpa said is true, the only ones who know it now are you and I. You're the first person outside the family to hear it, and I'm pretty surprised myself that I told it to you."

Ariel thought for a moment. "So you're related to one of those soldiers?"

"We all are, a little bit," she smiled, "but I guess so."

Then she went on. "My grandpa explained that this story was our family's legacy, and had been handed down from father to son for generations. My parents' accident had broken the chain, and it was up to him to teach it to me. When I asked him what that story had to do with my life, he replied I would have to find out for myself; that every Mader had to find their own way. All that he asked of me was that I hand the story down to my kids if I ever had any..."

"Talking of which," Ariel interrupted her, "we've, uh... *met* many times, but you've never told me your name."

"Sara Mader," she said, jokingly holding out her hand, "very pleased to meet you."

"The pleasure's all mine, Sara..." he replied, returning her smile.

Then he added "But you still haven't told me why you're a cleaner, and why you've suddenly appeared at my house this evening."

"I'm getting there," she reassured him, before going on. "Unfortunately, my grandpa died not long after, and I never got the chance to ask him any more about it. I had no-one left, and I forgot all about that story until something happened. A friend of mine, who worked as a cleaner in this building, told me she'd been sexually assaulted by a High Representative, who then threatened her, forcing her to quit her job. When she was telling me about it, she was so freaked out that she wouldn't even tell me the name of that pig. Just knowing that one of the spiritual heirs of that group of men my grandpa told me about had sunk so low, I decided to apply for her job, to find out who did this to her."

Everything suddenly clicked. "But this explains everything!" Ariel exclaimed. "Your suspicion towards me when you saw my medallion at the supermarket, why you were in Chandaha on the anniversary of the events involving your grandpa, why you ran when I chased you... and why, when you felt trapped, you gave me that kick in the balls I can still feel now!"

"I'm sorry," she said apologetically, looking him straight in the eyes. "You're the blameless victim of my greatest fears, and for that I apologize."

She looked away. "The problem is that a little while ago, my biggest nightmare came true - the same thing happened to me as to my friend, luckily with a very different outcome. So now there's another High Representative out there with excruciating pain in his nether regions, and I'm terrified that that maniac will do anything in his power to get back at me..."

She didn't have time to finish the sentence when the doorbell rang.

The two sat bolt upright and looked at each other in terror. "Quick, hide!" he whispered, pointing to the bedroom...

30. HONESTY

When the girl was safe and he opened the door, Ariel froze at the sight of Mandeo. Despite his best efforts to appear relaxed, the High Representative's pale features betrayed a sense of anxiety. His breathing was labored, and one hand was clasped to his side.

"Hey...what happened? You don't look too good," Ariel greeted him, trying his best to conceal his own amazement.

"A catastrophe! One of the cleaners has stolen a necklace from my lodgings. A family heirloom. It belonged to my mother..."

"So *he's* the pervert!" thought Ariel as an adrenaline bomb exploded inside him.

His world slowed and shuddered to a halt, as his mind chewed its way over the best recipes for roasting that pig's head in the oven.

It was only when he became aware of the clatter of his thoughts that he remembered Zimdar's words. "My young tyro," he had explained several days before, "many fools in the past have claimed that the end justifies the means. Now, I do not remember who was the first to write such an idiocy, but this phrase has been used to legitimize the worst crimes in history."

"You see," he went on, after one of his proverbial pauses, "shortcuts do not always take us where we want to go. The reason for performing a certain deed cannot survive if we betray it with our actions, because it is the tools that we choose for our project that determine what we can actually build."

In this particular case, if Ariel really had taken Mandeo's head off, as well as probably finding it empty, he would have ended up in prison, and despite ridding the world of that snake, he would have given free rein to the dark forces scheming against Populana.

And so, he limited himself to a shy "I'm sorry… is there anything I can do?"

"I'm going around the whole floor to see if anyone's seen or heard anything that might help me corroborate my account."

"I did hear a racket outside the door, like someone running away," Ariel replied, acutely aware how unconvincing that half-truth sounded.

Mandeo looked resigned. "That's what other people said, too. She's probably a long way away by now. I'll go and file a report with the police right away. Thanks for your help anyway."

"Don't mention it, you creep," thought Ariel, as he watched the most influential High Representative in Populana limp away.

31. REVELATION

Closing the door, Ariel called out to Sara, and without her saying a word, he sat back down in the corner of the room where they had begun to get to know each other. She looked at him, and moved by that tender gesture, she sat down next to him once more, the floor still warm from where they had been sitting just moments before.

"Thanks, you saved me," she said in relief. Then after a moment's hesitation, she began to speak. "I was doing the cleaning when that pervert came home. He was furious, cursing at someone who'd betrayed him. When he saw me, he pretended to be embarrassed and immediately said he was sorry.... initially he seemed like a nice guy, then he started giving me compliments about my body.... first about my butt, then my breasts... I tried to ignore him, but he came up to me and tried to unbutton my uniform... at that point I managed to struggle free and I hit him as hard as I could before I got out of there... all my stuff's still there, including the cleaning cart with my purse and my badge."

"That bastard…" Ariel muttered in a low voice. "I've got a bad feeling about this whole thing."

He was silent as the minutes ticked by, overcome by the events of that day and by all the emotions it had stirred up in him.

After a while, Sara ran her fingers gently along his arm. "Want to talk about it?"

"About what?"

"You said your day's been horrible… you've listened to me, and I'm here for you if you want."

Ariel was struck by the spirit of this girl, who was willing to help him despite the terrible situation she found herself in.

To his surprise, it felt natural to open up to her.

Although Zimdar would almost certainly reproach him for doing so, he told her everything. The Kurmar conspiracy, Razor's offer, Mandeo's disappointment following the result of the auction, Karen's strange behavior, and even his problems with Marianne.

Sara listened in silence, feeling a growing admiration for that boy she had so greatly underestimated.

When Ariel had finished, Sara confirmed "It's true, today Mandeo was absolutely furious and kept cursing about some Kostas…"

"Kostas?" Ariel was incredulous.

"Yeah, him… insulting him, calling him a crook, a dirty traitor… I don't know why…"

"Interesting. Come to think of it, that gigantic lardball wasn't with him tonight either, and in a situation like this I would've expected him to be right there, licking his boss's wounds."

"Just as well he wasn't," she breathed in relief, "otherwise I dread to think what would've happened."

"Right," Ariel agreed. "Mandeo's positively delightful in comparison."

Silence fell over them once more. Now it was Sara who began reflecting on the incredible turn of events: her own personal investigation and tonight's incident seemed almost insignificant compared to the enormous conspiracy that Ariel had stumbled into.

"I'm sorry this thing is affecting your career and your personal life, but for what it's worth, I think you're doing the right thing. It's our future that's at stake, and this whole affair is bigger than all of us. I know my grandpa would've liked you."

"Thanks Sara," Ariel smiled bitterly, "but the problem is that now Zimdar and I are at a dead end: we have absolutely no idea what to do next."

She thought for a moment, and suggested "If I were you, I'd call that woman Karen. You said you only told Zimdar what she said, when the decision to fire her had already been taken, so maybe she was fired for some other reason. Knowing why might give us an important clue."

"You might be right, Sara, it wouldn't hurt to try. Karen is Marianne's best friend, and I have her emergency number, I just hope she's not too angry," Ariel said, as he dialed her number.

When Karen answered, she was clearly drunk, and judging from the background music, she must have been propping up a bar somewhere, with only a strong drink for company.

"Whaddya want?" she muttered uncertainly.

"Karen, hey, I heard the news and I'm really sorry…"

"Shoulda thought of that before, you bastard!"

"Karen, I didn't tell anyone…"

"Yeah, sure, you men are all the same. I didn't mean it, Karen… It meant nothing to me, Karen… Karen you're my life…"

It was as if she was talking to someone else.

"She's completely gone," Ariel thought. "It's pointless trying to talk to her."

He was about to hang up when she went on. "Karen it was just a fling… Karen you misunderstood… Karen you got it wrong when you read those numbers…"

On hearing those words, something suddenly clicked. "Yeah, well, Karen, you sure fucked up when you read those statements!" Ariel retorted, mimicking the voice of Razor's director general. "How do you expect to run a company if you can't even read a bunch of numbers?"

Sara looked at him quizzically, before the bluff paid off.

"Listen you insignificant piece of shit, director general my ass!" Karen burst out. "I'm not stupid! I know what I read, and I know those statements showed a debt of three hundred and sixty million schlepps. I'm just sorry I didn't print those fuckers out, that way I could stick them up your ass and make you sing like a fucking cana…"

She was so angry, she cut off the call before finishing the sentence.

"I'm sorry Karen… but I had to know… I promise I'll make things right…" murmured Ariel in dismay.

"What does it mean? What's going on?" Sara asked, worried.

"That you were right - we're in major trouble!" he

replied gravely. "But we should get some sleep. You take the bed, and I'll sleep on the couch. Zimdar is a friend, but more than that, he's a wise man. He'll be here tomorrow at dawn, and he'll know what to do when this truckload of shit finally hits the fan."

"I sure hope so, my dear High Representative," she murmured, before going to bed with a glance that kept him awake well into the night.

32. WAKEUP

It was the annoying reflection of the sun on the walls that woke Ariel that morning. Sleeping on the couch had not been a smart move, and it was as if he had the hooves of some enormous goat digging into his back.

He turned on his side to dislodge the gigantic ruminant and tapped the Razor to see what time it was: 6:45 am.

"What the... why the hell didn't it go off?" he muttered incredulously.

That was weird: he'd set the alarm for 6:30 to give him time to prepare breakfast for Sara, but something had gone wrong.

"These damned slowdowns again…" he groaned, closing his eyes.

It must have happened just before the alarm was due to go off, preventing the device from sounding at the set time.

"This just gets worse and worse!" Ariel thought miserably. "The baboon that designed this thing must've swapped his bananas for some magic mushrooms! How the hell is it possible that the Tetron network, a system designed more than 300 years ago, works better than this piece of junk I carry around? It's gonna end up flying off the balcony before the day's over," he growled. "That should solve the problem once and for all!

"Not that you can really compare the two," he thought regretfully. "After all, it would take millions and millions of Razors to accumulate a power of calculation equal to that of the Tetrons…"

He stopped a moment to admire the orange light of the dawn filtering through his closed eyelids.

"Millions of Razors… Tetrons… flying…" he murmured.

The illumination arrived, accompanied by a jolt of adrenaline that swept away every last trace of sleep that had been lingering heavy in his limbs.

Wide-eyed, he sat down abruptly on the couch. "Of course! The 4357! Why didn't I think of it before? What an idiot I am!"

It was the din of his own voice that brought him back to reality: he found himself yelling under the quizzical gaze of Sara who had come out to see what it was that had woken her up.

"You can say a lot of things about you, but certainly not that you're an idiot," Sara greeted him, her face still fogged with sleep.

Ariel looked at her for a moment, astonished: with her tousled hair framing a beautiful smile, her natural, uncontrived beauty was bewitching.

"I'm sorry… really… did I wake you?" Ariel asked humbly.

"Don't worry," she reassured him.

Then she asked: "Have you thought of something?"

"Hold on just a sec.." he replied, putting his finger to his lips.

He tapped the Razor, brought it close to his face and said "Unblock", waiting for the familiar sensation of his skin as it stretched and then relaxed.

He went into the bathroom, set the device on the sink, and turned the taps on full to make as much noise as possible, before going back to Sara.

"You gonna tell me what's going on?" she asked him, intrigued.

"Of course," he reassured her.

"You haven't got yours with you, have you?" Ariel asked her, pointing to the patch of pale skin on her arm.

"No, I always take it off when I'm doing the cleaning. It's still on the cart in Mandeo's room."

"Okay," he replied. "As you know, the Tetrons communicate mainly by air. Although we've talked about underground forms of connection, the importance of the wireless traffic between the Tetrons is no secret to the people of Populana. But I suspect Razor is using the immense network of its own devices to illegally influence this flow of information. That would explain how it was able to modify its financial statements to win the auction for management of the electrical grid."

"Modify its financial statements? Are you sure? Have you got any proof, or is it just a hunch?" Sara asked him, perplexed.

"As I told you, I worked for Razor before becoming a High Representative. What I didn't tell you is that I was working on a solution to the slowdowns of the operating system due to the network code. Now, if we put together the recent increase in the number of these slowdowns, the sophistication of Razor's financial statements as reported by Karen, and the fact that these devices, owned by people all over Populana, have an overall power comparable to that of the Tetrons, I don't think there's any other explanation."

"Okay, I get it... but why have you put it in the bathroom?" she asked, puzzled.

"I don't know if I'm right, but if Razor is prepared to go to such great lengths to get what it wants, I don't think it's safe to speak freely when that damn thing's nearby…"

33. CONSPIRACY

The doorbell rang. It was 7:00.

"Hey Zimdar," Ariel greeted him, opening the door.

"Good morning young tyro… today it looks as if you have been run over by a truck! At this rate you will look older than me in a few days!" the old man observed, his expression a mixture of amusement and consternation.

"I had a terrible day yesterday, and last night I slept on the couch," Ariel replied, matter-of-factly.

"I hope you had a good reason - those things are dreadfully uncomfortable!"

"An excellent reason," Ariel revealed, pointing to Sara who was coming out of the bedroom at that moment.

"Please, come in," he invited him.

"Sara, this is Zimdar, my mentor, but most of all my friend," Ariel said, closing the door behind the old man.

"It is a pleasure, Sara," Zimdar replied. "I see you

have finally had the chance to meet this young man without injuring him too badly."

"The pleasure's all mine," she smiled, returning his affection.

They sat down at the table, and Ariel brought Zimdar up to speed on the events and the discoveries of last night, making sure to give an accurate account of the help Sara had given.

There was much to tell, and he talked for a long time. When he had finished, he was surprised by Zimdar's expression: he was sure he could hear the frenetic beating of his mentor's heart.

"Breathe, old man, or you're gonna have a stroke," Ariel joked.

"Thank you," Zimdar replied, regaining his usual composure. "You know, I have not always been old, quite the contrary. Many years ago, I was an impetuous young man just like you. Experience has taught me to control my emotions so as not to let them get the better of me. But no matter how determined we are, we must always renew our efforts to win the battles of the day before."

"I'd have loved to see you when you were a kid, beating up the dinosaurs," Ariel joked.

Zimdar smiled, before beginning his reasoning. "So to sum up, and correct me if I am wrong, the Razor Corporation has succeeded in doing what I thought was impossible - manipulating the memory of the Tetrons to modify its own financial statements. Developing this technology has probably taken years of work, and we were wrong when we thought that Kurmar had got there first: it turns out that Razor has been hard at work for some time. However, I think we can rest assured that the Larvini brothers do not have complete control: if they could influence the selection of the High Representatives or the administration of justice, we would not be here right now, talking about this whole affair. But now, having betrayed Mandeo, Kostas may inadvertently have put the last piece of the puzzle into place. With control of the electrical company now firmly in their hands, they will have the opportunity to study and manipulate the entire flow of information between the Tetrons. It may take some time, but this will allow them to gain absolute power over Populana, taking us back to a world of slavery that we thought had disappeared forever.

"In all of this, the beautiful young lady here," the old man added, causing Sara to blush ever so slightly, "has fallen victim to the perversions of Mandeo, who will almost certainly accuse her of th…".

The doorbell rang.

"Quick, hide!" Ariel whispered to Sara.

When the girl was safely hidden, Ariel opened the door.

"Sergeant Coss Molo of the Populana police. Mr. Ariel Nat?"

"Yes, that's me."

"We have reason to believe that a woman called Sara Mader, suspected of theft, is hiding here in your lodgings. We are here to take her into custody. It is my duty to inform you that if, in this instance, you should provide false information regarding her whereabouts, you shall be punishable in accordance with law 0001-112. I also wish to inform you that, given the overwhelming evidence in our possession, if you should deny that the woman is here, it will only take a few minutes to obtain a warrant to search your apartment. Now, I shall ask you once only. Is Sara

Mader here in your lodgings?"

The hulking sergeant paused, waiting for a reply, which did not immediately arrive. Ariel felt the words clog in his throat: while he could not risk ending up in prison, he detested the idea of handing over the girl.

"Sir," said Coss, swelling like a toad, "I need an answer."

Ariel stammered "I…"

At that moment, Sara, who had heard everything, came out of the bedroom. "I'm here."

Ariel was on the point of doing something incredibly stupid, when Sara came up to him, took his hand, and murmured: "Don't."

The sergeant put a pair of handcuffs around her wrists, and giving her a tablet, announced "You are under arrest. Pursuant to law 0001-92, you have fifteen minutes to examine the accusations that have led to the curtailment of your personal freedom. I would also like to inform you that if you should try to tamper with the handcuffs, or to escape, you will be neutralized with an electric shock."

"I will wait for you here outside," he added, stepping outside the door. "Come out when you are ready to go."

Ariel, who had taken Sara's hand once more, leaned in towards her, and together they read the words on the screen of the tablet. "No way!" the two exclaimed in unison.

"What does it say?" asked Zimdar, who had not spoken up to then.

Ariel took the tablet and read aloud. "Following the charges brought against unknown subjects by Mandeo Gutt for violation of law 0001-314 against property, and in the presence of elements of proof that place said Sara Mader at the scene of the crime, the magistrate ordered a search of the lodgings of the suspect, pursuant to law 0001-113. Having found in said lodgings an object which corresponds exactly to the description of the stolen necklace, Sara Mader is ordered to be placed under arrest. Rub Etti, the prosecution lawyer drawn for this trial, has declared his willingness to conduct the proceedings in abbreviated form. The victim's statement, supporting evidence and cited laws are given in the attachment."

"This is more serious than I thought," Zimdar said, frowning.

"It's not serious, it's false!" Ariel burst out. "She's been with me all night! Even if she was guilty, how could she have taken the necklace home?"

"Control yourself!" Zimdar retorted. "I know that you care, but you are not helping her like this!"

Then he turned to Sara and asked her: "Do you know the necklace that they describe?"

"No," she answered, glancing at the photo. "I've never seen it in my life, and have absolutely no idea how it ended up in my house!"

"Good," the old man replied. "So, someone must have put it there."

Then he added "Ariel's testimony will have no value at the trial, given that it cannot be circumstantiated. We must prove it was not you who took the necklace to your house. Do you have any idea how we could do that?"

Sara thought for a moment, and replied hesitantly "Perhaps there is a way. I live in the semi I inherited from my grandfather. When he died, I needed money, so I sold one of the two houses. My new neighbor, Ortiep Nob, is a great guy, and we get on really well.

He just has a couple of weaknesses: he always turns his music up way too loud, and he's just a little bit paranoid, one of those people who thinks everything's a conspiracy, and who'd go around wearing a tinfoil hat if he could. Lately some idiot has started throwing electrical components into our yard: little things like switches and bits of cable. I guess it must be some electrician who uses our yard as a garbage bin on his way home from work. I don't really care: I clean up and don't think anything of it. But for Ortiep it's become a matter of life or death. He thinks it's proof of who knows what planetary conspiracy, and he's filled our yard with microcameras that film non-stop. If anyone has gone into my house, Ortiep's footage should have caught them."

"Give me the address, I'll go over there right away!" Ariel offered hopefully.

"It's not that simple, unfortunately - he doesn't know you, and he's extremely wary of strangers. But if you still have the groceries from that day at the supermarket, there might be a way."

"I think I've eaten nearly everything - I didn't have time to go back to the supermarket that day," Ariel said apologetically.

"Even the Tormu?" she asked, incredulous.

"No way! That stuff's gross... I'd rather die young than eat that swill!" Ariel replied, taking the packet out of the kitchen cupboard.

"Excellent!" grinned Sara. "Ortiep is convinced that regular food like bread and cheese contains additives put there by the State to control our minds. So he only eats Tormu, but being a niche product, it's only sold in bigger stores like the one at the High Chamber of Populana. The Tormu I bought that day was for him."

Grabbing a pen that was lying on the sideboard, she wrote 'Out of toilet paper, eh bro?' on the package of Tormu.

"Give him this, he'll understand," she said, giving it to Ariel.

"Good," Zimdar interrupted them. "All is not lost!"

Then he turned to Sara. "Time is running out and they are going to take you away. I am not your lawyer, but if you have faith in this Ortiep, I advise you to accept an abbreviated trial, that way the proceedings will be over by the end of the afternoon. We cannot afford to wait until the end of the month, given that Razor is inching its way closer to the Tetrons, and may soon have control over the administration of justice…"

Coss knocked at the door. The fifteen minutes were up. Sara leaned in close to Ariel, kissing him on the cheek as she took the tablet from his hands. "Thanks, it means a lot."

Then she walked to the door and said resolutely "I'm ready. Let's go."

Ariel watched her leave, escorted by the police officers, as he softly stroked his cheek: he could still feel the lingering warmth of that kiss.

34. ORTIEP

Sara's house was in a residential neighborhood just behind the tracks used for the Intelliraces, the most popular sport in Populana.

When the High Chamber banned Intellimobiles from the roads, the Brainzo company found itself with warehouses full of cars that had nowhere to go. To pay its suppliers, to whom it owed a great deal of money, the company began selling the vehicles at knockdown prices for use on private land. This led to the cars being employed for a whole range of purposes, until a certain Brandon Krutt decided to create a competition where teams of programmers pitted their vehicles against each other over an obstacle course.

Since then, these modified cars had lost most of their resemblance to the original models, and all that was left of that remote past was the name of the sport.

"It must be a safe neighborhood when there aren't any races on," Ariel thought to himself, hiding his medallion in his pocket just in case.

He rang the doorbell, but no-one answered. All he could hear was the loud noise of what many young people in Populana called music.

He tried again, but the result was the same.

Overcoming his indecision, Ariel climbed over the gate to go and knock at the door. He was almost halfway up the path when an enormous mastiff sprang out of a corner and ran towards him barking.

The music stopped almost immediately and a voice yelled from the window. "Get him, Blue! Don't let him get away!"

Ariel ran towards a tree in the middle of the garden and scrambled up it just in time to avoid being bitten.

The same voice, closer now, rejoicing in triumph. "Good boy, Blue! Got that coward at last! We're gonna make that sucker sing!"

Still clutching the tree, Ariel called out blindly. "Please call your dog off, there's been a mistake... I'm just a friend of Sara's and I... I can't sing!"

Peals of laughter followed. "Do you really think I'm that stupid?"

"I can prove it! I've got a gift for you... but... call off that monster... I'm begging you!"

"Throw down the present first," the voice said suspiciously.

Ariel dropped the pack of Tormu and the boy ordered: "Bring it here, Blue... good boy, let me see..."

After a moment's silence, he burst into fits of laughter. "This toilet paper thing again! It only happened once, but she won't let it lie!"

Then he added "You could've told me right away you're a friend of Sara's. Come down, don't stay up there in that tree like a baboon in heat!"

Ariel cursed him silently as he climbed down from his refuge, and when his feet touched the ground, he glanced worriedly at the animal still growling from behind his master's legs.

"Don't worry, bro, he's harmless," the boy assured him, proffering his hand "Ortiep Nob, pleased to meet you."

"Ariel Nat, the pleasure's all mine."

"How is Sara? I haven't seen her for a while…"

"Not that great, to be honest. She's been arrested."

"Yeah, I heard, bad news bro, I saw the cops this morning before dawn. I've told them a million times there's something major behind all that weird stuff in our yard!"

"Right!" Ariel said, playing along. "That's why I came: I'm convinced those creeps came here to frame her, and I need the footage from last night to prove it."

"Come on, bro," said Ortiep, resolute. "Let's go inside. Those assholes' days are numbered!"

They went up the steps and into the house.

The living room was a pleasant mixture of styles. Two modern loudspeakers stood guard, like diligent soldiers, on either side of an antique wooden unit, which held an enormous screen.

"Welcome to my world," Ortiep said proudly.

"This place looks amazing!" Ariel said approvingly, admiring the titanic concentration of technology.

"Yeah bro," Ortiep replied in satisfaction, "this whole system cost me a ton of schlepps, but it was totally worth it, though I dunno if the neighbors would agree …"

Then, fiddling with the remote control, he added "Problem with all these recordings is I never have time to watch them. Shall we start at five yesterday evening?"

Ariel thought for a moment and nodded. "Yeah, that should be okay."

Ortiep announced in a loud voice: "Play the video surveillance recordings starting from five pm yesterday. Synchronized mosaic. Fast forward 3 times," and twelve frames immediately appeared on the screen, each showing footage from a different microcamera.

"Have a seat," he said, pointing to the large brown armchair, "this is gonna take a while."

It was exceedingly boring. Nothing happened. The height of the action was someone walking past the gate, a few cars speeding past, Blue chasing a cat, Blue resting, Blue barking, Blue going into the house for dinner. Then nothing.

More than an hour had gone by, and Ariel was on the verge of falling asleep in an uncomfortable haze of monotony, when a yell jerked him awake. "There he is, the brute! Camera six full screen!"

"What the hell is he yelling for? We've been watching that damned dog for the last hour!" Ariel thought irritably, before realizing that Ortiep was right. A dark figure could clearly be seen opening the gate and coming in.

Suddenly the man passed by the yard light, illuminating his face for an instant. It was Mandeo, holding the keys that Sara had left in his lodgings.

"That sneaky bastard!" exclaimed Ariel, bristling with anger. "Can you make me a copy of the whole clip?"

"You bet!" Ortiep replied, and after scolding the dog for not having bitten the intruder, he downloaded the footage onto a memory card.

When he had finished, he held it out triumphantly. "I knew there was something behind all this! Make sure he gets what's coming to him!"

Ariel nodded and thanked him over and over, secretly blessing him for that absurd obsession of his. Their chances of saving Sara were looking brighter than ever before.

35. JUSTICE

Ariel got to the court at two pm sharp: the trial started in an hour, and he was just in time to give the evidence he had acquired to Do Lin, the lawyer drawn to represent Sara.

Their meeting lasted as long as a handshake. Now all he could do was wait: he would only see Sara at the hearing.

He sat down on an armchair and looked around. The offices were teeming with life, and everyone seemed very focused on whatever job they were doing.

"Just as well the justice system isn't what it used to be," he thought, remembering the words with which Zimdar had reawoken him from his kiss from Sara. "It won't take long," his mentor had consoled him with a hand on his shoulder, "Populana's justice system is very efficient."

Then, as usual, the old man had been unable to resist his usual sermon on the past. "You see, before the Great War, things would have looked very bleak for Sara. Today, when you are accused of a crime, your lawyer is chosen at random, to give you the same chance as anyone of being defended by someone who does their job well or who does it badly. Things were different before the war: you had to pay for the services of a good lawyer, and the better they were, the more they charged for their services. In other words, justice was administrated based on the contents of one's wallet, and if you add the unequal distribution of wealth, you can truly understand what kind of places the courthouses were back then."

"Alright, but didn't the judges and politicians do anything to make the justice system fairer?" Ariel had asked.

"You have to remember that the government system of the time put the role of the magistrates and that of the politicians in direct competition with each other, in a permanent war of prohibition that took the respective privileges of each side to the extreme..."

"You mean the politicians and magistrates used their power to engage in childish power games, and that this made the justice system more unfair for ordinary people?"

"Precisely! Today, with the random selection system, an attorney can no longer choose who to prosecute, and politicians, being regular citizens fulfilling a temporary role, have no interest in reinforcing a position they will only be occupying for a year. But this is not the only reason why the justice system works better now. You see, here in Populana, the entire trial is based exclusively on the ascertainment of the crime. To order a trial, the prosecution must produce between one and three different, complete, and unequivocal pieces of evidence that the law has been broken. The proposed sentence is applied in a manner proportional to the number of pieces of evidence that the defense is unable to invalidate. If one remains valid, the defendant is sentenced to a third of the maximum proposed sentence: to two thirds if two remain valid, and if three remain valid, he must serve the entire sentence, given that he has almost certainly committed the crime. This asymmetrical structure makes trials extremely brief, their revision too, if one or more pieces of evidence are invalidated. So although the criteria for examining evidence are much more restrictive, and arrests less common, the number of crimes that go unpunished is much lower, since the courthouses are no longer clogged with trials based on some flimsy pretext. Before the war, on the other hand, justice was administered in a summary manner, and trials based on circumstantial evidence were the order of the day. The situation was also aggravated by the fact that the court would try to guess what was in people's hearts and minds, and punishments were inflicted based on how convinced the judge was of the degree of malice, and of the severity of the crime."

"What do you mean exactly?"

"To give you an example, if the judge believed a defendant to be in a mentally incompetent state at the time of a murder, this would guarantee him a much shorter sentence, while if he was convinced that the crime was premeditated, his sentence would be more severe…"

"But that's absurd! Surely the point of the sentence is to rehabilitate the person found guilty? Someone who can't control themselves is much more likely to offend again: they shouldn't be getting a discount!"

"Indeed," Zimdar had continued, "but the point is

that the trials at that time resembled interminable sessions of psychoanalysis of the defendant, tangling themselves around an idea of blame closer to divine justice than to that of men. If you kill a person, you have extinguished a life, and it does not really matter if you did so deliberately or not. Distraction certainly is not a better reason than hatred to kill a man. The only thing that matters for the purposes of human justice is if the deed has occurred or not. It may seem cruel, but there is no judge on Earth who can lessen the gravity of a murder. Also because judges are human beings, and as such are not devoid of emotions, and they can take decisions based on feelings: indeed, it is no coincidence if today the result of any trial is determined by a majority vote of three judges, who read the same transcription of the trial at the same time, isolated from each other and from the courtroom. They are not even permitted to know the name of the defendant, which is redacted from the text. Without counting the fact that only those who succeed in passing all the twelve feared tests of objectivity can become judges…"

"We can produce all the evidence we want, but judges are still human beings at the end of the day," Ariel had observed, still worried about Sara.

"Of course they are," Zimdar had replied. "Their training helps, but what really makes the difference is the principle of the three pieces of evidence, forcing all parties involved to focus exclusively on ascertaining the facts. It is for this reason that trials today are no longer inconclusive theater performances that hang round people's necks like an albatross."

"Sure," thought Ariel, gazing at the clock on the wall. "The justice system has come a long way. Let's just hope it works in Sara's favor."

36. TRUTH

The trial began in fifteen minutes, and it was time to go in. After a final moment of hesitation, Ariel got up and timidly stepped over the threshold of Allesia's courtroom number four, where Sara's fate would soon be decided.

She was there, at the bench on the left together with her lawyer, while on the right sat the prosecutor Rub Etti. In front of them was the empty seat of the moderator with the stenographer alongside, also known as a pianist due to the strange keyboard used to transmit the report to the judges. Further back, on one of the benches provided for the public, sat Mandeo, who shot Ariel a withering glance.

Zimdar arrived shortly afterwards, breathing heavily, and sat down next to Ariel.

"Run a marathon, old man?" Ariel joked.

"No, I've spent the last few hours at the archive, looking through the old news reports for a photograph."

"Did you find it?"

"It took a while, but yes I did."

"What's this about?"

"We will talk about it afterwards," whispered Zimdar, indicating the comical-looking man who was settling into the central seat in the courtroom.

The moderator announced "The court will now proceed against Sara Mader, with the charge 346-1564 for violation of the law 0001-314 on property. It should be noted that the parties have agreed to an abbreviated trial, foregoing the period of thirty days to prepare the case. I wish to remind those present that we are here solely and exclusively to determine whether or not Sara Mader has committed the crime of which she is accused. Evidence that is equivocal, incomplete or circumstantial is not admitted in this courtroom. Testimonies with no supporting evidence are likewise prohibited. The report, the laws in question, and the charges brought against the defendant are shown on the screen at your desks. Each party has the right to request a fifteen-minute suspension of proceedings. For the entire duration of the session, the defendant is not permitted to leave the courtroom. The prosecution will now read the description of the events as reported by the victim."

Rub Etti stood up and cleared his throat. "Declaration of Mandeo Gutt, victim of the crime. At six thirty pm, as I was returning peacefully to my lodgings, I heard suspicious noises coming from the bedroom. I immediately went in, and found a cleaner rummaging through my wardrobe. When I asked her what she was doing, the woman attacked me, then ran off. Later, as I was looking through my wardrobe, I saw that the necklace (described in Annex B), a family heirloom which belonged to my poor late mother, was gone."

Mandeo did not pass up the opportunity to adopt a severe and satisfied expression.

The moderator nodded, and when Rub Etti had sat down, declared "The defense, if it so wishes, may now read the declaration of the defendant Sara Mader."

Do Lin stood up and spoke in a clear voice. "Declaration of the defendant Sara Mader. I was diligently doing my cleaning job in lodging number 82 of the High Chamber, when the tenant Mandeo Gutt suddenly came in. He was agitated and seemed angry with someone called Kostas. When he became aware of my presence, he immediately apologized and seemed very kind. Then, however, he began making sexual remarks about my body and tried to remove my clothing. At that point I managed to struggle free and I fled. Having left my house keys and my purse on the cleaning cart, I was unable to return home. I therefore decided to take refuge in another lodging on the same floor, that I knew belonged to a boy I had previously met at the supermarket. I spent the whole night there before being arrested by the police."

In hearing those words, Ariel was surprised to feel a sense of happiness, knowing the girl had deliberately chosen his apartment. She had gone where she knew she would be safe: that meant she had looked for him before their third encounter.

He wondered if and how often she had been watching him, and if it had been her that day in the elevator. He imagined Sara going in to his room all alone, and the thought excited him so much that for a moment he forgot all about the gravity of the situation.

The moderator's voice brought him back down to Earth. "The prosecution may now inform the court of the number of distinct, complete and unequivocal pieces of evidence it wishes to present."

"One," replied Rub Etti laconically.

"For sure," thought Ariel, "it can't have been easy to find other evidence, since there aren't any cameras inside the lodgings for reasons of privacy. And since Sara often goes there to do the cleaning, her fingerprints on the wardrobe wouldn't count as unequivocal evidence."

The moderator went on. "Let it be noted that the trial will be based on the discussion of one single complete and unequivocal piece of evidence. The prosecution may now describe the evidence in its possession."

Rub Etti got to his feet once more and began to speak. "I will now proceed to announce the first and only piece of evidence of this trial. As you can see from the police report on your screens, a necklace corresponding to the description provided by the victim when he reported the crime was found during the search of Sara Mader's lodgings. The correspondence was verified by technicians 4, 9 and 43 of the courthouse. As further confirmation of the fact that the stolen item belongs to the victim, the necklace bears the fingerprints of Mr. Mandeo Gutt and is identical to the jewelry worn around the neck of his mother in a photograph that he himself has provided. It should be noted that the search was carried out in accordance with current legislation, and was authorized by the magistrates following the discovery of the defendant's personal effects at the scene of the crime. The discovery of the stolen item in the defendant's home leaves no room for doubt: she and she alone stole the necklace and hid it in her lodgings."

Ariel turned to observe Mandeo who wore an expression of grim determination, nodding rhythmically almost as if to substantiate the prosecution's words.

But he soon tired of that miserable spectacle, returning to gaze at the shoulders of Sara, who was fidgeting nervously in her seat.

"Just as well the judges can't see them right now," he thought. "Mandeo is extremely convincing, while Sara looks terrified."

After Rub Etti had sat down, the moderator spoke again. "The defense now has the right, if it is able, to invalidate the evidence presented by the prosecution."

Do Lin stood up. "I now proceed to invalidate the first and only piece of evidence presented by the prosecution. As you can read in the report authenticated by technicians 14, 36 and 71 of this courthouse, the surveillance cameras located in the yard shared by Sara Mader and Ortiep Nob, neighbor of the defendant, incontrovertibly show that Mr. Mandeo Gutt entered the home of Sara Mader shortly after the presumed theft, using the keys that my client had left in his lodgings when she fled. I wish to stress that the address of my client is registered in the Razor device she left in her bag as she fled from her attacker's apartment. I also wish to point out that the only fingerprints found on the necklace were those of Mandeo Gutt, not those of the defendant as you would expect if the latter really had hidden the item in her lodgings. I therefore believe we can affirm that my client did not place the necklace in the location where it was found, and I ask that this evidence not be considered valid for the purposes of determining the sentence."

He sat back down with a satisfied expression, as a mask of fear spread over Mandeo's face, replacing the disappointment that had been there before.

The moderator leaned in to the microphone. "Discussion of the evidence is at an end. The judges may now express their opinion. I stress that no-one may leave the courtroom until the verdict has been issued. Make yourselves comfortable, this will take some time."

While Rub Etti and Do Lin had honored the good name of their profession, demonstrating the fruits of the long nights spent ensuring that their texts were logical and concise, the judges appeared to be in no hurry whatsoever to examine the evidence.

More than an hour went by, and the wait was excruciating, especially for Mandeo, who seemed to be regretting his decision to watch the proceedings.

Just when those present in the courtroom were settling into that surreal, wordless limbo that always precedes an important event, the moderator spoke. "I will now proceed to announce the verdict. Three judges out of three have deemed the proof presented by the prosecution as insufficient to reach a verdict. There is no evidence that the defendant Sara Mader has committed the crime. Therefore, she is free to go. Any additional elements that have emerged during this trial will be evaluated at a subsequent time. The session is concluded!"

For a moment the courtroom seemed bigger, divided as it was between the contrasting feelings of those present. The relief of Ariel and Sara was immense as they hugged each other, her feet barely touching the ground in delight. Time to grab his cane, and even old Zimdar joined them in an explosion of happiness that had the sound of Mandeo's hasty escape.

"Enough of courtrooms for today!" Ariel exclaimed, taking Sara's hand. "Let's go and celebrate: I'm buying!"

The three walked towards the exit, giddy with the joy that only a well-deserved victory can bring. Unfortunately for them, that happiness was to be short-lived.

37. STORM

"Mr. Ariel Nat?" asked the sergeant Coss Molo, who was waiting for them with another two officers at the exit of courtroom number four.

"Yes, that's me, we already met this morning," replied Ariel in surprise.

"You have to excuse me, but in my job it's always better to ask twice," said Coss by way of explanation.

"What can I do for you?"

"I need you to hold out your hands."

Ariel was too shocked to disobey, and before he could reply, Coss put on the handcuffs that had been on Sara's wrists just that morning.

Then he said: "You are under arrest. Pursuant to the law 0001-92, you have fifteen minutes to examine the accusations that have led to the curtailment of your personal freedom. I would also like to inform you that if you should try to tamper with the handcuffs or to escape, you will be neutralized with an electric shock."

He handed him the usual tablet and moved away.

A stunned silence fell over the group. It was Sara who first found the strength to speak. "Don't stand there like an idiot! Read it! What are they accusing you of?"

Ariel read aloud. "Following the financial checks performed to ascertain the ability of Ariel Nat to re-pay the damages he caused by flooding his apartment, it has emerged that Mr. Nat accepted a transfer of funds from Novalit United, in open violation of law 0001-12 relative to the High Representatives' Code of Conduct. In the light of such unequivocal evidence, Mr. Ariel Nat is ordered to be placed under arrest. Vang Miur, the prosecution lawyer drawn for this tri-al, has declared his willingness to conduct the pro-ceedings in abbreviated form. The statement, sup-porting evidence and cited laws are given in the An-nex."

"What an idiot I am!" exclaimed Ariel. "I forgot to turn off the tap that I turned on to stop the Razor in-tercepting our conversation. It's been on all day!"

"Dammit young tyro, where is your head?" thun-dered Zimdar.

"Control yourself!" Ariel mimicked, finding a shred of good humor. "I know that you care, but you are not helping me!"

The three broke into a bitter smile that vanished as quickly as it had appeared.

The old man spoke. "Obviously you do not have the faintest idea what Novalit United is. I imagine that Razor is closing the net around us: it must have used its data-modifying abilities to get at you. It knows we know, and is prepared to do anything to stop us inter-fering."

Ariel nodded. "Time's running out: the longer we

wait, the worse it'll be. We have to stop them!"

"Yes, but how?" chorused Zimdar and Sara.

Lost in thought, Ariel was silent for a moment. Then, looking down and ventured "Maybe there is a way."

He was silent once more, before raising his eyes to meet those of his friends. "I'm not proud of what I'm about to say, but… see, uh… when I worked at Razor, I developed a really deep hatred for Charlie Baid, an idiot colleague of mine, who as well as getting on my nerves, seemed to have made it his mission to undermine everything I did. Unfortunately, my boss Toss Sterling always agreed with everything that fat ass did, and Charlie could persuade him to do anything in that slimy way of his."

He paused again before continuing. "I had a lot of good ideas for the company, but with Charlie always there, I was never able to get them past management."

He gazed at the floor again before going on. "One day, I couldn't stand it anymore, and I created a computer virus to sabotage him. The plan was to install it on his workstation as soon as he was away from his desk. That virus would have corrupted the end product of his work, inserting lines of code that would have saturated the processor usage for various minutes. So, at the next major update scheduled for the end of the month, every Razor in Populana would freeze up for a fair while. And the company would be forced to withdraw that update and fire my colleague… at least that was my plan before I got the Call."

Ariel lifted his gaze and apologized, visibly contrite. "I know, I know… I did an awful thing, and I deeply regret it. But I can't change who I was. I can only say that after everything I've learned in these last few days, I'd never do it again."

Zimdar and Sara looked at him, their eyes filled with sympathy more than condemnation.

The old man spoke first. "I have made many mistakes in my life, and if people judged me on those alone, I would be in a fine pickle. I have seen with my own eyes the presumptuous lad that you were become a young man, intelligent and sensitive. If I ever had to depend on someone, that someone would be you."

Sara added "Ariel Nat, I knocked you down twice and treated you like dirt. You should have hated me, but you helped me when I needed a hand. I don't know who you were and I don't care. All that matters is who you are now."

Ariel was deeply moved, and his companions with him.

Zimdar brought them back to reality. "Let us get to the point, time is running out. I do not understand how your virus can help us, given that Razor can cancel the update."

"See, here's the thing," Ariel replied. "Under normal conditions, the operating system has a protective mechanism that prevents this type of error from overloading the processor for more than a few seconds: this prevents overheating and breakage of the Razor. But for specific programming needs, such as when you want to test the potential of new experimental hardware components, you can give the development environment a command that overrides this type of security mechanism. If the modified software is compiled in this way and reaches the devices, it'll fry them beyond repair before anyone can stop it. There are a couple of problems, however…"

"What problems?" Zimdar asked.

"First, the virus is on a memory card in the central pocket of my suitcase in the bedroom. I'm under arrest so I can't go and get it. Second, the suitcase is on the floor, so it might have been irreparably damaged by the flooding."

"It's your lucky day!" Sara exclaimed. "First, thanks to you, I'm a free woman, one who has her cleaning job back, with access to all the rooms, including yours. Second, it was pretty messy around your bed, and I couldn't help cleaning up a bit: I put your suitcase on top of the wardrobe."

This time it was Ariel who planted a kiss on her cheek, as she joked, smiling. "Happy to be of use!"

Ariel, serious once more, added "But there's one other massive hurdle. That virus will only destroy all the Razors if someone can insert the memory card into Charlie's computer before the update. That person will also have to press the square and triangle keys and the letter D simultaneously on the code screen to disable the protection flags in the development environment…"

Zimdar's face darkened. "And how in the devil's name do we do that?"

"I hate even the mere thought of what I'm about to say," Ariel replied, "but Charlie has two weaknesses. His horrible obsession for that pimp DJ Tarmac, and his crazed hormones that keep him glued to chatrooms for hours, in search of a soulmate."

He swallowed and his voice caught in his throat.

Sara was more encouraging. "Don't say anything. You helped me, now it's my turn to help you. It's not you that's asking me to do this: it's me that wants to do it."

"Are you sure?" Ariel asked in a small voice.

"Absolutely. It doesn't matter if it takes a bit of time. I'll go to Novardia and I'll find a way to get to that console, whatever it takes."

"Alright," Ariel replied, his face clouded with worry. "His username is 'TarmacSuperLover1114', and you'll find him in the 'Desperately Seeking Love' chatroom on the 'Lonely Hearts' dating site."

It was Sara's turn to swallow.

Zimdar nodded. "Good, let us hope it works. This is our only chance. In the meantime, I will do everything in my power to get you out of this mess."

"Thanks, Zimdar, but I don't hold out much hope this time," Ariel replied, disconsolate.

Zimdar replied: "Hope springs eternal, my young tyro, but now you must listen to me. I have something very important to tell you: it concerns my visit to the archi…"

He didn't have time to finish the sentence when Coss approached. "I'm sorry, but your fifteen minutes are up. I can't play favorites. Time to go."

Ariel took Sara's hand, but only had time to say "Be careful," before he had to leave, following the sergeant as he miserably prepared to meet his fate.

38. BROTHERHOOD

"Oh man, I'm in major trouble," thought Ariel as he waited, head in his hands, in custody room number five. Even if Tim Coan, the lawyer he had been assigned, was the best Allesia's courthouse had to offer, he certainly would not have been able to confute a piece of evidence that came directly from the Tetron network. The sums that entered the account of each citizen were never accredited until the account holder gave his consent. In this case, Ariel knew he had not authorized the transaction, but the sum resulted as having been transferred, violating the principle of neutrality that expressly prohibited the High Representatives from receiving money during their mandate. Society took care of providing them with everything they needed, to prevent them using their vote for personal gain.

Misfortune, in this circumstance, had robbed Ariel of the time to react. The financial checks were normally carried out when taxes were collected at the end of each trimester. The same rate was levied on all citizens and companies, calculated based on the amount of money needed to replenish the State funds to the levels prescribed by law, up to a maximum of 20% taxation. If this did not suffice, a duty was applied to all those citizens richer than 95% of the population. If that still wasn't sufficient, the threshold dropped to 90%, and so on and so forth, until the target was reached. For Populana, in fact, it was of vital importance to keep that shared wallet well-stocked, the very same one set up by the founding fathers when the country's currency was created. Indeed, it was these funds that were used to cover all of society's costs every three months.

Ariel could still remember what Zimdar had told him in Chandaha: before the war, the economy had been completely turned on its head, and all the countries were heavily in debt. No family could ever have survived at the mercy of loan sharks, with debts that exceeded 100% of their earnings. The system was completely disconnected from reality, and he couldn't understand how those people could think they were free.

"If you have to ask other people for money every time you need something, you end up being their slave," Ariel thought in bemusement.

It remained a mystery how men who applied that principle in their daily lives could think that society worked in a different way. They thought nothing of denying the people their freedom - one of the very conditions required for democracy.

But it didn't stop there. The government was under the influence of those who held the greatest concentrations of wealth, and who refused to apply a policy for its redistribution, another condition needed for democracy. Democracy simply isn't possible when there are individuals in society who hold great power.

"The reason's pretty simple," he thought, "the Representatives have to reckon with these powers before and after being selected. This means that their government isn't the expression of a common will, but of the same fat cats who accumulated wealth at the expense of others."

There was no way out, it was the proverbial dog chasing its tail: a dog with more than one owner, feeding off the selfishness of all those, rich or poor, who yearned to have more than others.

Ariel finally began to understand the importance of 'brotherhood' - the most underestimated, and often unspoken condition necessary for democracy.

"It's wonderful that society has managed to rid itself of all the madness that used to pass for an economy," he reflected, "but none of this is much help to me right now. Maybe at one time, with the right lawyers, money, immunity, and all the other politician's privileges, I might be a free man right now."

Unfortunately, in this case, there was no way out. The financial checks had shown that he, Ariel Nat, had accepted a transfer of money from Novalit United during his mandate as High Representative. There was nothing for it. The Tetrons never lied, and he was sure to rot in prison.

39. TIM

When Tim Coan arrived, he didn't take long to confirm to Ariel that the situation was desperate. "I've read the accusations and I'll be honest with you: trials like these are a foregone conclusion, and unless it's a case of mistaken identity, we don't have much hope of confuting the evidence."

"I know." Ariel sighed bleakly.

"I advise you to refuse an abbreviated trial," Tim said. "Perhaps some other information will emerge over time, although the chances are pretty slim."

"It wouldn't make much difference: actually, I'd rather it was all over as quickly as possible," he said, fearing that Razor might have other surprises in store. "At least in prison I'll be safe," he thought.

"Are you quite sure?" Tim asked, concerned.

"You can bet on it," Ariel assured him.

"As you wish," said the lawyer in resignation.

Then he asked "I know that you've recently requested plumbing repairs in your lodgings: is that correct?"

Ariel nodded.

"Although it serves no purpose for the trial, given that the notitia criminis was obtained in good faith, I'll have them check if the recent repairs had anything to do with the flooding. Maybe I can save you a bit of money. There's really nothing else I can do."

"Thanks Tim, though I doubt it'll do any good, since I'm the one who left the tap running," Ariel said bitterly, before withdrawing into himself.

He stayed there, in that room, until the time of the trial the next morning. When the sun rose over the horizon, they came to collect him and took him to courtroom six, and he crossed the threshold with the resigned air of someone who already knows the verdict.

The prosecution was only able to produce one piece of evidence, and Tim did everything he could, even risking being thrown out for presenting arguments with no objective basis.

There was nothing for it. Despite steeling himself for the verdict, Ariel's heart sank when he heard the moderator pronounce his sentence. "I will now proceed to announce the verdict. Three judges out of three have deemed at least one piece of evidence presented by the prosecution as valid for reaching a verdict. There is one and only one complete and unequivocal piece of evidence that the defendant has violated law 0001-12. The court of Populana therefore sentences Ariel Nat to two years imprisonment, to be served at the Ronin correction facility. The session is concluded!"

As Ariel realized the weight of those words, an invisible spear ran through his stomach, the pain causing him to double over slightly. Two years was an infinity.

When he turned around, he saw his own suffering reflected in the face of Zimdar, who had watched the entire proceedings. The yell of the old man, that "Hang in there Ariel, I'll come to visit you!" as they took him away, was lost in the noise of the traffic of Allesia, as the guards transported him towards the Ronin correction facility.

40. MORA

For Sara, getting into Ariel's room was easier than she had anticipated. When she arrived for work the morning after the arrest, the supervisor Mora Pal didn't think twice about assigning her the cleaning of the flooded apartment. For once, her supervisor's contempt came in very handy.

Coming into the apartment, she looked dismally at the terrible aftermath of the flooding: the dampness, the furniture swollen at the bottom, the marks on the walls just above the skirting boards, the dirty floor. It looked like the inside of a house after a hurricane.

The very first thing she did was rush into the bedroom to check the suitcase. It was still on top of the wardrobe: her natural love of tidiness had saved it from damage, and she had no trouble finding the memory card. Although Mandeo seemed to have gone to ground, she somehow did not feel safe putting that tiny treasure in her purse that had been in his hands, and she slipped it carefully into her bra.

She spent the next few hours trying to sort out the

apartment as best she could. Time passed peacefully: there was only one moment of panic when the door opened around midday, and a couple of men came in, followed by a comical-looking elderly man in dungarees. They explained they were there to establish whether the recent repairs had had anything to do with the flooding, and at a certain point, while the others were busy with their various measurements, the old handyman approached her and introduced himself. "Joe Plum, ma'am. Sorry to bother you - I wanted to ask if you know anything about the kid who was living here. I hear he's in a bit of trouble."

Wary, Sara decided it would be better to pass that particular hot potato over to Zimdar. "Sorry, I don't know much. You should talk to Zimdar Kun, his mentor. But you'd better be quick, because he's only at the High Chamber for a few more days."

"Thank you kindly," Joe Plum replied, and Sara felt a flash of guilt at the old man's sincere interest.

Soon the men left, and Sara continued her work. It took her almost the whole afternoon, but she was proud of the result Although the damage was still visible, the lodgings were both habitable and incredibly clean.

When she had finished, she went straight to the supervisor's office.

"Forget it!" Mora Pal retorted. "No way am I giving you so much time off. You know we're short-staffed!"

"Hey, I've just been attacked in one of those rooms!" Sara protested. "It's too soon for me to come back to work: today I tried, but I keep getting these awful flashbacks…"

"Sorry. I hear you, but it's out of my hands," her

supervisor replied sourly, folding her arms.

Sara felt her fury rise. With all the holidays she had accumulated, and with everything that had happened, she wasn't about to take no for an answer. Suddenly she could no longer contain her anger. "Listen, either you give me the days I'm due, or I'm just gonna take them, and then you'll have to find someone else that works as hard as I do, and who doesn't answer you back like you deserve!"

For a minute, the two women were silent, both taken aback by that unexpected reversal of roles.

Mora Pal thought for a moment, and threw up her hands in resignation. "Alright, you've got three weeks. But if you don't knuckle down when you get back, you can find yourself another job."

"Thank you!" Sara breathed, before leaving the office in delight. Now she had all the time she needed to help Ariel.

41. TOM

The prison guard Nel Sent rubbed his eyes and thumped the screen a couple of times to make sure his eyes weren't deceiving him. No, there was no mistake. The monitor showed beyond a shadow of a doubt that Ariel Nat was to be housed in cell 444B.

"I don't get it! That cell's never used! Old Tom won't be pleased…" Nel grumbled aloud.

Then he picked up the Intercom and called Tom Maz, the first floor cleaner. "Hey Tom, there's a prisoner here for cell 444B."

"What the…? You been on the bottle? You quite sure?" growled the old cleaner, incredulous.

"Absolutely. Checked it twice. Even rebooted the system, but no joy. The system's got its heart set on 444B, ain't nuthin' gonna change its mind…"

"Dammit! Well this is a first. You know we only use it as a storeroom! It's gonna take at least three hours' work to clear it out and make it habitable!"

"I know, Tom, I know, but you know the rules. There's nothing I can do."

The old man grunted and hung up without saying goodbye.

After a last incredulous glance at the monitor, Nel turned to Ariel and the guards accompanying him. "Make yourselves comfortable. Cell 444B ain't ready, and won't be for the next three hours. The system's drawn a cell that's never been used in the last twenty years, so we always used it as a storeroom. You know what these damned Tetrons are like. Always doing whatever the hell they want!"

Four interminable hours passed before Ariel finally set foot in his cell. Barely larger than a regular room, it had a bed, a sink, a toilet, a desk, and a shower. A small barred window was the only point of contact with the outside world.

It was only when the guards closed the heavy cell door with its spyhole, the only way in and out, that Ariel realized the irrelevance of that four-hour wait compared to the two years he was going to have to spend in that hole.

42. KURMAR

The first two days of his detention were the hardest. Ariel had absolutely no desire to do anything at all: he spent them lying on his bed, limp as a rag, crushed by the hand Fate had dealt him.

It was only a visit from Zimdar on the third day that finally roused him from his slump. As soon as he came in, the old man realized how well he had done to keep his promise: at the sight of Ariel, completely overwhelmed by the events of the last few days, he felt his heart plunge in his chest, triggering a twinge of paternal instinct.

"My young tyro," he joked, "I have never in my life seen anyone look so wretched for having received two million schlepps!"

Ariel, who had not heard him come in, opened his eyes in delight. "Zimdar!"

He sat up on the bed, and after a long, slow stretch, recovered some of his old spirit. "Not that there's much to joke about, you know very well they won't let me keep the money. If I'd known earlier, at least I would've spent it!"

Zimdar looked at him in relief, happy that his spirit had survived that terrible ordeal.

"I'm so happy you kept your promise!" Ariel said gratefully. "Any news?"

"Not much," Zimdar replied. "Sara found what she was looking for in your room and has gone to Novardia…"

"Sara…" Ariel murmured, a ripple of anger pushing away his misery. "Just the thought of what I asked her to do disgusts me…".

"Do not worry," the old man said reassuringly, "Sara is a smart girl. She will be fine."

"And what about you, Zimdar? Your time at the High Chamber's up, right?"

"It is indeed. My mandate ended the moment you were sentenced. As far as the system is concerned, I have failed as a mentor. The seat will remain vacant until a new Representative is drawn."

"And who'll teach the new Representatives now that you're gone?"

"The Tetrons will draw another mentor from the names of those who have already completed their mandate," the old man replied.

"I see," Ariel conceded with a sigh, shaking his head. "Did you manage to finish your research at the archives? We never had a chance to talk about it with everything that's happened."

"Yes. That is precisely what I wanted to talk to you about."

The old man was silent for a moment, as if collecting his thoughts, then he began to speak. "Almost fifty years ago, during the celebrations for the three hundredth anniversary of the Republic, the High

Chamber decided to renovate the historic monuments of Populana. During the work inside the Tetron of Allesia, the first one ever constructed, the three large inscriptions on the inside walls were removed, and behind that of Brotherhood was a strange inscription, showing a hexagon inside an equilateral triangle. Since I was working at the university at the time…"

"Ah-ha!" Ariel interrupted him. "You were a history professor! So that's how you knew all that stuff…"

"You are wrong," Zimdar replied mischievously. "I was only in charge of the archive. Very often there was no work to do, and I would read to pass the time…"

"The devil makes work for idle hands and all that, eh Zimdar?"

Zimdar could not help but laugh before continuing. "As I was saying, I remember this story because the discovery led to a very heated debate, and for once, the archive was full of academics who wanted to solve the mystery. Sadly for them, all that commotion did not lead to anything of substance: some theorized a connection with the ancient symbol of the Eye of Providence, also known as the eye of God, the protector of humanity. Others suggested a connection with the hexagonal symbols of Latropp's party, and interpreted it as a warning. Most thought it was a meaningless scribble, a pastime of those who had worked the stone. The latter theory was also substantiated by the unique nature of the carving, which had not been found anywhere else. The inscription was soon put back up, and no-one has talked about the matter since. Even for me, after all this time, that figure was little more than a faded recollection, and I had immense difficulty finding a photograph in the news reports that could refresh my memory."

"Interesting anecdote, but I don't see what it has to do with us. Why are you telling me this?" Ariel asked, perplexed.

"That memory came to mind when I was observing the sign on the back of your neck on your first day in the Chamber. That hexagon, the one tattooed on your neck, has come back to haunt me on a number of occasions, and I truly thought I was becoming obsessed. At the time I did not understand why, but I had the feeling that it was important. And this feeling was confirmed when you explained that you got it inside a Tetron."

"Sorry, I still don't understand what you're getting at," Ariel broke in with a frown.

"Well, pyramids are often stylized as triangles, and it was inside a pyramid that you got that hexagon on your neck. I do not think it is a coincidence. That engraving was only found in the Tetron of Allesia, and I am convinced that, for some reason, the founding fathers are telling us that you must go there…"

"Forgive me, Zimdar, but it looks like my jailtime's gone to your head!" Ariel joked. "It's a bit of a stretch, this theory of yours - this mark on my neck was just bad timing, me sitting on that VR chair just when Kurmar was playing God with the power supply…"

Zimdar nodded. "That is what I thought too - it is a habit of mine to doubt every theory, and there have been times when I believed I had gone completely insane. You know, I am old and I must be careful."

"You can say that again - sometimes I wonder if you took a bomb to the head during the Great War!"

The old man smiled before going on. "I thought

about the matter a lot after your trial. And I realized that in order to understand whether or not I really *was* going mad, I would have to investigate Kurmar. After all, it was these outages that first raised our suspicions, along with the mysterious accident you had at the precise moment you were sitting on one of their chairs. To me it seemed impossible that the founding fathers had given a private company so much power over the Tetron network. So, I did some research on the company and on who has been managing it for generations. And I discovered a number of interesting things. Kurmar was founded in the year 0001, and has been run by a member of the Naltop family ever since. The family goes back over three centuries, and is extremely reserved - its members never appear in public, and almost nothing is known about them, apart from the fact that every administrative direct of Kurmar, including the current one, has always taken the name of Patron Naltop. All of this made me think: what if the latest Patron Naltop, member of such an honest and devoted family, had decided to betray them? Having had the means and the opportunity for more than three hundred years, why has none of them ever tried to do it before? It was a frustrating few hours, spent leafing through information without getting anywhere, until, re-reading the texts in the archive for the umpteenth time, I found myself repeating the name of Patron Naltop, over and over. And it was then that I noticed something curious. Patron Naltop is an anagram of Anton Latropp."

Ariel tried rearranging the letters and was stunned - if his jaw hadn't been firmly fixed in place it would have clattered to the floor.

"You're right! How weird!"

Zimdar nodded. "I think the founding fathers had a sense of hu…".

The old man was interrupted by a sudden start from Ariel, who leapt to his feet as if fired into the air by one of the mattress springs. "Kurmar. Kur-Mar. They're the first letters of Kurzi and Marvan, the two rival factions who buried the hatchet to set up Populana!"

Now it was Zimdar's turn to remain open-mouthed. "By Jove young tyro! Have you been brushing up your history over the last two days?"

"No, just lain here like a slob," Ariel admitted. "Actually, it's all thanks to the story of Sara's grandpa, and her for telling it to me. It had details about the Foundation of Populana that I don't think you'll find in any books, but out of respect to her, I think she should be the one to decide whether to tell you or not. There must be a reason if the story's never been told before."

"Very well," Zimdar replied, his curiosity aroused. He would almost certainly have given his right arm to know more, but it was right that Sara be the one to decide whether or not to reveal that family secret.

After a short pause with both of them deep in thought, Ariel began thinking aloud. "Let's say we were wrong and that Kurmar was created by the founding fathers, a product of the Tetron system. This would mean that the outages could be benevolent, maybe a response to Razor's attack on the network that had been going on for months. We also know that Kurmar was interested in ownership of the electrical company too, and that it used Mandeo's thirst for power to get it. I'm absolutely convinced of this, otherwise they'd never have made such a large offer, and our friend wouldn't have been so furious when Razor duped them. There are two possibilities at this point: the first is that the VR chairs are somehow relevant to the functioning of the Tetrons, and the second is that maybe Kurmar needed more power to protect itself. But this rash move has given Razor an advantage it could use to destroy Kurmar."

Zimdar nodded in agreement. "I fear that the system underestimated the greed of the Larvini brothers and the control they had already gained over it. In any case, I am convinced that we will find the answers when we go into the Tetron of Allesia."

"Sorry to have to jog your crumbling old memory yet again, but it'll be another two years before I get out of this hole," Ariel objected bitterly.

"Do not fear, my young tyro," Zimdar replied enigmatically. "Sometimes even old people do stupid things..."

Just then the siren sounded, announcing the end of visiting time. Although those forty-five minutes of conversation were already up, they had breathed new life into Ariel. When Zimdar had gone, he tidied his cell and took a shower. He had finally re-discovered the will to live, and had just one thought on his mind. Sara...

43. VIRUS

As Ariel had predicted, it hadn't been hard to tempt Charlie. To his colleague, finding a woman willing to put up with more than three minutes of chat about DJ Tarmac and how sexy his groupies were had seemed too good to be true.

After leaving him on tenterhooks for a while to whet his appetite, Sara had given in to his pressing requests to meet, and they had arranged a date at Bar Tendi. Sara had then taken the train to Novardia, where she had rented a hotel room.

Dressing and doing her makeup exactly like DJ Tarmac's girls had been fun, but any sense of pleasure evaporated as soon as she stepped out of the hotel: the cold air hitting her bare legs and gusting under her tiny miniskirt immediately made her feel extremely uncomfortable. And when she felt herself being undressed by the gaze of every man in the neighborhood as she walked into the bar, she was engulfed by a deep sense of shame.

Although that aggressive look certainly wasn't her

style, it worked like a charm, and Charlie's suspicious nature melted like ice-cream in the sun. They immediately began seeing each other, and after a week and a half, using various excuses, Sara had managed to visit him three times at work, where she learned he was working on an important update for Razor.

Her rapid progress soon hit a wall, however, since the lumbering lardball never left his workstation, and his boss, Toss Sterling, did not look kindly on family members dropping in.

But that wasn't all: over the last few days, Charlie's requests for sex had become increasingly insistent, and the night before, Sara had come dangerously close to having to comply. Although she had absolutely no intention of having sex with that slimy individual, he had given her an ultimatum, and to appease him, she had begun to undress, fighting down the urge to retch. But lucky for her, it was all over as soon as she had taken off her blouse and bra.

"Thank God for premature ejaculation!" she thought, as Charlie made a hurried excuse to bring the evening to an end.

His hasty departure, however, clearly showed just how little he trusted her. "If two people really care about each other, they work together to overcome hurdles like these," she had said to herself as she went home, definitive proof that no matter how many parallel universes existed, she and Charlie could never have been a couple in any of them.

Those thoughts kept her company in the long sleepless night that followed, and it was in utter desperation that she walked to the Razor building the next morning. And when Toss shot her a withering glance when she came into the office, Sara was convinced that her luck had finally run out.

She went over to Charlie and kissed him on the cheek. He stank like a wild boar, as if he hadn't washed in a week.

"Hi, I brought you a snack... I'm really sorry about how things ended last night," she said, holding out a paper bag.

"Yeah, well, we'll try again tonight," he replied, expressionless, his eyes never leaving the screen where he was typing the source code.

A shiver ran down Sara's back. "I'm a bit tired, I'm just gonna sit down here a sec," she said, unaware it was Ariel's chair she had chosen.

"Whatever, just don't stay too long otherwise Toss'll be pissed," Charlie retorted, showering his console with crumbs from the sandwich she had brought.

At that moment Sara realized why Ariel detested him so much. He hadn't even thanked her, and had simply announced that they were to have sex that evening - he had no consideration for her whatsoever. DJ Tarmac, by comparison, busy fondling a girl on Charlie's new desktop wallpaper, was a true gentleman.

Seconds later, Toss stood at Charlie's desk. "Just to remind you that the update's for this evening," he warned. "Need you to finalize those last modifications for quality control, ASAP. We're behind as it is - hardly the time to be fooling around with your girlfriend."

A few minutes after Toss's warning, Charlie began to show signs of irritation, and Sara realized it was all over. He was about to kick her out, and she wouldn't be able to carry out her plan.

She had failed, and who knows how long it would be before she had another chance. Maybe weeks. Or months… that evening she would have to choose between throwing in the towel or giving herself to that gigantic human slug for who knows how long. If she gave up, all hope would be lost for Ariel and for Populana. If she chose to go on, she would be literally crushed, as a person and as a woman, ruining her life forever.

She felt completely lost, but Charlie, who barely glanced in her direction, did not notice the terror in her eyes. He began to say "You have to go, otherwise T…" but was interrupted by a strident voice coming from the parking lot.

"Direeeeeectoooor? Director freaking general, you dickass piece of shit?"

After two milliseconds, Toss was at Charlie's desk, visibly excited. "Charlie, you have *got* to see this! Karen Tanf, that bitch of a vice-director who was fired? She's down in the parking lot, blind drunk!! She's drawn an enormous flaccid penis on the director's car, and she's doing a striptease, yelling obscenities into a megaphone!"

"Wait here!!" Charlie ordered Sara, leaping to his feet with an unusual agility. "This is for men's eyes only!"

The office emptied in an instant. Everyone was literally glued to the windows, laughing, yelling, urging her on. It was like a gaggle of orangutans watching a truck full of bananas pass by.

"Thank you, Karen," Sara breathed. "This is the second time you've saved our lives. Ariel and I and the whole of Populana owe you everything," she thought, as she inserted the memory card and watched as the virus opened and closed various windows.

When that choreography come to close, she returned to the code screen and pressed the combination of keys as Ariel had instructed her to do. The computer returned a beep of confirmation, and for an instant, the words 'Hardware Protection Disabled' appeared on the screen.

At that very moment, building security managed to placate the poor Karen Tanf and took her away. The show was over, and the animals trailed back to their cages. Sara just managed to remove the memory card and move seats before Charlie was back.

Her heart was thumping as if she'd just run a four-minute mile, but the big chump, in his excitement, was completely oblivious.

"Still here?" he grunted.

"Oh yeah, sorry, I'll get out of your way," she said, straightening the chair.

"Can I take this dinosaur?" she asked to distract his attention, pointing to the little soft toy sitting on top of the adjacent screen.

"Be my guest, it belongs to that idiot colleague of mine," he replied. "If you get it out of my sight, you'll be doing me a favor."

Sara picked up little Zico and left in delight.

It was over. That little dinosaur had brought her luck, and she would never have to spend time with that lewd moron again. She would return to Allesia that very evening.

44. LIGHTNING

After Zimdar's visit, Ariel's days in his cell became a little easier. Their discussions had given him a new thirst for life, and he had begun organizing his days as if he was a free man. He would get up early in the morning, work out doing press-ups and crunches, then have a shower and wait for them to bring his breakfast.

To his great surprise, the food wasn't bad at all, since the authorities had long since realized that good food kept prisoners in much better spirits. When he had finished eating, Ariel would read the news of the day. As soon as his father's severe criticism, his depression, or the disgusting image of Sara crushed by Charlie's flabby body began nudging their way into his thoughts, he would go back to working out, before throwing himself on to the bed in exhaustion to reflect on the events of the past month.

Among his favorite topics of thought, after Sara and all the things they could do together, there was Zimdar's theory of the symbol that Ariel had nicknamed "The Eye of the Tetron". Although the old man's bizarre theory had more holes than a fishing net, the more he thought about it, the more convinced he became that it was their only hope, tenuous as it was. And when you are in jail, with no prospect of getting out any time soon, hope becomes faith, and having a purpose is the only way to survive that terrible ordeal.

This was how Ariel spent his days, in that monotonous daily grind, with nothing to disturb his forced condition of tranquility.

The premonitory signs of the storm that would sweep away that frustrating flat calm came one morning, when after his workout he noticed a delay in the arrival of his breakfast. That perfect machine of shifts, men, and everything that made up the Ronin correctional institute seemed to have jammed.

And when later, reading the news, he learned that the whole of Populana had ground to a halt due to a breakdown of its Razor devices, Ariel was unable to contain a yell of triumph. "Awesome, Sara! You did it!"

Reassuring the guard who had come to check on him, Ariel read to the end of the story. During the night, all Razors had begun heating up beyond the threshold of tolerability, to the point that the fixing mechanism in Reptiflex had been disabled for reasons of safety.

Apart from a few mild burns, there had been no serious consequences for its users. The same could not be said for the personal assistants themselves, which had melted and now lay like helpless pools of molasses on the floors of homes all across the country. With the demise of the device that almost everyone used to organize their days, Populana had woken in chaos, with great inconvenience for its citizens.

Ariel's enthusiasm, however, began to wane when he read the press release in which Razor, after profuse apologies and the announcement of having fired the employee responsible, assured its customers of having the necessary funds to guarantee the rapid replacement of all devices free of charge. Soon, Sara's efforts would all have been for nothing, and to his great surprise, Ariel even began to feel sorry for Charlie, who had lost his job for no reason.

His mood worsened even further when he read, in a brief article relegated to the bottom of the page, that the custodian of the Tetron of Allesia had noticed strange numbers appearing in random order on the screen of the large Gaudion machine. Despite replacing various components, the problem still had not been resolved.

They had come to the end of the line; Ariel could feel it. Razor was just a step away from victory.

45. THUNDER

The longest workout in history wasn't enough to banish the sensation of imminent defeat that crawled into bed with Ariel that night.

He lay there for a long time, wondering if his inability to sleep was due to worry or to exhaustion. There were times that he was too exhausted to sleep, but this was different: he was alert, not weary.

It was nearly midnight when he began to feel drowsy, falling into a lucid dream in which he was chasing Sara along the streets of Chandaha. She had just run past the armored tank, and had taken refuge in the lobby of the building that was in the sights of the gun.

He had just caught up with her: he knew that scene like the back of his hand. Him pouring with sweat, her approaching him despite her fear.

"So why are you following me, Mister High Representative?"

"Well, if you hadn't run off, you might have found out earlier…".

"So, are you gonna explain what you're doing here?"

"I came for my groceries."

Ariel braced himself to receive the greatest physical pain he had ever felt in his life, but Sara, instead of kicking him, leaned in and whispered in his ear. "Get out of the way."

"What?" he asked, stunned.

"Move, kid!"

At that moment, he heard a dull explosion from the gun behind him, and felt a violent shove to his back and a blow to his face.

When his lungs finally managed to take in air once more, Ariel opened his eyes, recognizing the floor of his cell in the weak light coming through the window.

He pushed himself up on his hands and knees.

"What the hell...?" he muttered, noticing a huge black hole in the wall.

He edged closer for a better look, when a rather disturbing looking dummy appeared in the hole, who hissed "Take it!" Ariel fell backwards in fright: this was the weirdest dream of his life.

"Quickly, for Pete's sake!" the dummy whispered irritably.

Ariel lay there, dazed, watching that curious-looking dummy bobbing around in the hole.

At that point, the stuffed head whispered "Hey Zimdar, you sure the kid hasn't lost his marbles in his cell somewhere?"

"I am not sure he had too many to begin with," an even fainter voice replied in amusement.

"Zimdar?" Ariel stammered, incredulous.

"Come on kid, move it! It's Joe Plum, and old Zimdar is down below. We've come to get you out, but if you pussy-foot around any longer, they'll be banging us up in here with you, and you'll have us for company during yard time!"

"What the hell are you doing in the wall?"

"There's no time for that now! I'll explain later. Come on, grab that darned dummy and stick it in the bed before the guards get here!"

Ariel did as he was told, wrapping it in the sheets, before slipping into the hole and sliding downwards for about ten feet, holding on to the walls to slow his descent, until he felt his feet touch the ground, and recognized his old mentor in the weak light of the torch he was holding. Towering above them was a dark passageway, emanating a foul smell.

As Zimdar hugged him, Ariel realized that the old man himself was the source of that awful stink. "Oh man, Zimdar, you forgotten how to take a shower?"

"Well, since we must now go through the sewers, you will soon smell worse than me!" his mentor replied mischievously.

Joe Plum dropped down beside them, having closed the hole in the wall using an ingenious fixing system.

"That should do it," he whispered, unaware that a guard was inspecting the cell through the spyhole at that very moment: the only reason they hadn't been caught was that Ron Tarz, the man guarding the first floor, had paused for a few moments before tearing himself away from the latest episode of the Intellirace Extravaganza.

"We do not have much time!" Zimdar urged them. "Come, the Tetron of Allesia is waiting for us."

Joe went over to an enormous vertical pipe with a diameter of around forty inches, indicating a large opening leaking sewer water. "Good thing not many people use the toilet at night, otherwise we'd be wading through a sea of shit," he smiled before ducking inside, immediately followed by Zimdar.

Ariel joined his two friends in the hole: the pipe ran downwards into the ground for about four feet, then curved at almost a right angle, sloping imperceptibly.

He squinted into the darkness but could barely see a thing. Below them was a trickle of damp filth that he fervently hoped was from some leaking pipe somewhere.

They crawled dozens of feet on their hands and knees, away from their point of departure. The going was tough: it was extremely slippery, and Zimdar was struggling. Behind him, Ariel had to stop often, marveling at the courage of that old man who normally walked with a cane. To him, crawling through this sewer must be like climbing a mountain, yet he had somehow found the strength to be there.

After about seventy feet, the pipe opened into a much bigger conduit, where they could walk upright.

Having put some distance between themselves and his cell, Ariel decided it was finally safe to speak. "You wanna tell me how the hell you knew about this escape route?"

"I bet if we don't tell you now, you're gonna bug us all the way to the Tetron," Joe teased him.

"You better believe it," Ariel said firmly.

"Okay, well… as you know, when I worked at Modelbyte, I was stupid and arrogant. I loved taking risks and I was completely hooked on gambling. About twenty years ago, the day I was given the task of programming the robot that was to create the Ronin correctional institute, it was the final of the Intelliraces, and I was so determined to watch that damned race that I didn't bother re-checking the project. It wouldn't have taken much to notice the problem, but I didn't. The error was forgivable: about point nine of an inch less in the width of each individual cell, but the project was enormous, with four hundred and forty-four cells per floor. The result was an air gap on one of the two sides of the institute, which they ended up incorporating into the sewer system. There was a major scandal, and I lost my job. I never thought this whole business would ever come up again, until the day Sara suggested I talk to Zimdar, and I found out you were being held in that very same prison. So, I told Zimdar to check the number of your cell. And I was pretty surprised to discover they'd put you right on the perimeter: a massive stroke of luck!"

"I do not think it is a question of luck," Zimdar interrupted him. "I may be wrong, but we will find out this evening."

They walked in silence for a while, until they came to an iron ladder which led to the surface.

Their wet hands and feet offered little grip on the rungs, and the climb was exhausting. Zimdar almost slipped twice, but Ariel caught him from behind.

"Going down was easier," the old man complained, when he finally managed to drag himself out of the manhole with the help of his two companions.

When they reached the outside, Ariel stopped and took a long, deep breath: the cool night air in his nostrils had the sweet smell of freedom.

46. IMPULSE

There was a car waiting for them, with Sara at the wheel, who immediately returned Ariel's affectionate gaze.

"Jump in! Hurry!" she called to them, rolling down the window.

It didn't take her long to regret the invitation: the stink was nauseating.

"You guys smell gross! Hope you don't care about your seats too much, Joe..." she said with a smile.

The old handyman grimaced, as he took something from under the passenger seat.

At the sight of the shiny cylinder, Ariel asked "Is that what I think it is?"

"Yup, a modified MEV," Joe replied. "At first impact, it'll release an electromagnetic impulse strong enough to turn off any electronic device in the range of a whole block for a few hours. It'll neutralize the surveillance cameras so we can get close without being seen..."

"Let's hope it doesn't switch the Tetron off too," Ariel said in concern.

"Do not worry, young tyro, if it was so simple to

disable the Tetrons, Razor would not have needed to hatch such an elaborate plan to sabotage them," Zimdar replied, as Sara started the engine.

The streets were deserted. Everyone was sleeping, and not a soul stirred. The car sped through the streets towards the center of Allesia, when all of a sudden, Sara glanced worriedly it the rear-view mirror.

"They're following us!" she exclaimed in horror.

"Who?" Joe asked in alarm.

"I don't know, but there's someone behind us."

"Turn right, now!" Zimdar commanded. Sara did as she was told, the tires screeching, but the car was still behind them.

"Take a left here!" Zimdar ordered her.

Again, that sudden maneuver proved useless: the other car was still on their tail.

"Try again. Turn left then pull in!"

This time, the old man's advice worked. The other car carried on, followed at a distance by a vintage motorcycle, a rare sight these days on the streets of Populana.

All four breathed a sigh of relief and resumed their journey. The Tetron was close by, and it wasn't long before they were at their destination, parking the car behind a building at the foot of the rise where the great illuminated pyramid stood. When all four of them were out of the car, Joe covered it with a shiny tarpaulin he took from the trunk.

"I've always dreamed of doing this," he said with a grin, before throwing the modified MEV hard into the distance.

For a moment nothing happened, then suddenly all the lights went out simultaneously.

"Good!" Joe said, satisfied with his handiwork.

"The surveillance should be disabled. Let's go!"

They climbed the hill in long strides, with Zimdar out of breath and lagging behind. They were almost at the entrance when, to their horror, a large figure stepped in front of them.

"Stop right there, all of you. I'm armed," Kostas Bull warned, a metal object in his hand that glittered in the pale light of the fading slice of crescent moon.

Zimdar, who had arrived breathless at that very moment, shouted a warning. "Look out! That's a weapon from the Great War! Unlike the police weapons, that thing can kill!"

At that moment, Kostas Bull recognized Ariel. "Well, well, well. And what have we here? A fugitive! Looks like this is my lucky night!"

Then he turned to Zimdar. "As soon as I saw you talking to that ridiculous handyman in dungarees, I knew you were up to no good. You hate technology. Everyone knows you're just a senile old man who can barely use a cane. You had no reason to meet that guy all those times. I was right to keep my eye on you!"

"I'll show you what I can do with this cane!" Zimdar growled.

"Put that crazy old man on a leash, or I'll do it for you!" Kostas shouted in fury. "It's over. I'm in charge now. Move and I'll shoot. The police will be happy to arrest a criminal and his accomplices. We just have to wait until the surveillance system comes back on. With all of you in prison, we can finally finish what we started…".

"Vicious lowlife!" Ariel burst out. "If you think you can scare me by waving that ancient lump of metal around, you can think again!"

He went to take a step forward, but stopped at the

sound of a metallic click coming from the weapon. "Don't force the future director of Razor to shoot you. I'd rather take you alive, but I'll do what I have to. It's over. Give yourselves up, you've los…".

Before he could finish his sentence, a huge branch crashed against the back of his neck. The blow was so powerful that the wood snapped with dull crack.

Kostas crashed to the ground, and a voice started shouting. "Dirty traitor… director my ass! You were nothing and I took you under my wing. Is this how you repay me? Giving all our secrets to Razor for a miserable job as director? You're nothing but a dirty bastard!"

The four could barely believe their eyes. It was Mandeo. Obsessed by Kostas' betrayal, the High Representative must have spent his time at large following him, until that evening when his suspicions had finally been confirmed.

"My neck…" moaned Kostas, still conscious despite the blow and struggling to stand up.

"Hurry, let's go in!" Sara shouted, pointing to the entrance that was now free of obstacles.

Ariel put his arm around his old mentor's shoulder, and the four hurried inside.

"Gently, my young tyro, or you will break me in two!" the old man protested, as an enormous black slab descended, sealing the entrance behind them.

"Where the hell did that come from? I didn't know they could close!" observed Ariel in awe.

"Nor me… never seen anything like it…" Zimdar replied weakly.

He was sure of it: never in the history of Populana had a Tetron ever closed that way…

47. TRUST

"Look!" exclaimed Sara, pointing to the monitor of the Gaudion. From a distance, the large screen seemed to be filled with little dots, flashing on and off.

"Looks like the system's gone mad!" Joe observed in amazement, as the whole image formed itself into a large hexagon.

The three approached to get a better look, and noticed that the figure was made up of an endless series of tiny numbers. "One zero six," Sara read, squinting at the screen. "Four seven seven five eight one zero six four seven seven five eight... it's the same number, 10647758, repeated over and over. It doesn't make sense!"

Ariel held out his arm in the light of the screen so that everyone could see. "Yes it does, it's my identification number!"

At that moment, they heard two shots and a dull thud from outside.

"Quickly, Ariel, do what you have to do!" Zimdar

urged him, pointing to the large niche that had just opened in front of him.

Ariel approached and stepped inside the cavity to identify himself.

The machine recognized him, but suddenly seemed to freeze, and began obsessively repeating the same three words. "Welcome Ariel Nat... Welcome Ariel Nat... Welcome Ariel Nat...".

"It's completely gone..." murmured Joe in dismay.

"By Jove, we are in trouble! Let us go to the Chamber of Brotherhood, maybe we are still in time!" Zimdar commanded.

They dashed into the second room, but when Ariel sat on the Kurmar VR chair, nothing happened.

"Let's hope it's not too late," he said in alarm, sitting down once more. But again, nothing happened, the only sign of life from the system was the Gaudion machine which continued to heckle him from the room next door.

"Let us try to move the inscription," suggested Zimdar, pointing to the huge slab bearing the word 'Brotherhood'.

All four pushed with every ounce of strength they possessed, but the mass of rock refused to budge even a fraction of an inch.

"Let's go to the third room," Sara said suddenly. "Maybe we'll find the answer there."

Joe nodded. "Nothing left to lose, I guess."

In the Chamber of Freedom, the screen above the console showed the same hexagon with the same identification number.

Ariel quickly pressed the button 'Accept'.

"Nothing!" he said, crestfallen.

"Try the other one," Joe suggested.

"I hope it's not the wrong choice. But at this point, I don't think we've got any other options," he said, and pressed 'Refuse'.

Still nothing.

"So that's it," he said miserably. "We've tried everything. Razor probably succeeded in damaging the Tetron beyond repair before we could do anything."

Zimdar, who had been silent up to then, suddenly spoke. "We have not tried everything. You can press the two buttons at the same time. As absurd as it may seem, accepting and refusing at the same time is the equivalent of choosing not to choose. This is the same decision that our fathers took when they abandoned the elections forever, putting their fate in the hands of men chosen at random. It was like giving a minimum part of their vote to all the others, whether friends or enemies. Now, if you press those two buttons together, you annul your judgment and you entrust yourself completely to the women and men who founded Populana. This loyalty, the blind faith in humanity, is the cornerstone of democratic religion and the very reason for being of the Tetrons themselves!"

"It does make some kind of sense…" Ariel thought, as he pushed down on the two buttons: to the amazement of everyone, a voice immediately began repeating the same ominous words coming from the Chamber of Equality, and the phrase "Welcome Ariel Nat…" now bounced from one part of the Tetron to the other.

They then returned to the Chamber of Brotherhood, and Ariel sat down once more in the Kurmar VR chair. With a gentle hum, the antenna with its six elements arranged in a hexagon positioned itself against the tattoo on the nape of his neck.

He flashed a last smile at Sara, before the familiar voice of the chair led him gently into a new world.

48. POPULANA

Ariel opened his eyes, but saw nothing. It was a dark, moonless night; a faint breeze caressed his forehead and carried an acrid smell of smoke to his nostrils.

He turned slightly and saw a glare in the distance. He began walking towards it, stumbling over rocks and rubble, until he reached a tree.

Ariel leaned against the trunk to catch his breath, observing the scene. A group of men were warming themselves around a fire in front of a sinister armored tank.

Suddenly a girl turned round and spoke. "Don't stand there in the cold. Come, Ariel Nat. Come and sit with us."

He approached warily and sat down next to her, watching the flames dancing in the wind, before he finally plucked up the courage to speak. "Who are you?"

The men and women replied in unison. "We are Populana."

The eerie sound of those voices speaking as one startled him, and it was a while before he found his voice again. "Are you the founding fathers?" he asked.

This time only the girl spoke. "Them and all the others. We are the community."

"The c...community?" he stammered.

At that moment the fire and the armored tank exploded, transforming themselves into a vast sea of people. Ariel was floating over millions and millions of faces, gazing at him, their expressions frozen.

He felt a hand on his shoulder and a familiar voice. "We are all the people who have inhabited Populana ever since its foundation."

Ariel turned and recognized his grandmother, who he had lost when he was still a boy.

"But... but how?" he murmured.

Just then, the people at his feet began to billow outwards, turning into buildings. Ariel found himself flying over Allesia, and saw thousands of people connected to their Kurmar VR chairs in their homes.

"What does it mean?" he asked, disorientated, addressing old Joe Plum who in the meantime had taken the place of the elderly woman. "Kid, your theory that the electrical grid puts the Tetrons in communication with each other was only partly right. See, what it does is connect all the people of Populana through space and time... the calculating power of the Tetrons is boosted by all the minds of the people who sit in the Kurmar VR chairs every day. Every time someone connects to the network, their intelligence fuses with that of all the people throughout history who have ever lived in Populana. The choices made by the Tetrons are none other than the combined result of the mind patterns of all the citizens of our nation, past and present."

"But you would need an enormous storage capacity to contain the minds of all those people!" Ariel interrupted him skeptically.

"You're not looking at this the right way," the handyman said. "You don't need two ponds to contain two waves... a person's thought is triggered by a series of impulses and by their interaction. The Tetron network is the result of the continuous interference of these signals, that bounce from one chair to another through the electrical grid. To put it simply, it's as if people were the neurons of an immense brain that holds the great mind of Populana."

"Amazing!" Ariel exclaimed. "Hold on, though," he continued, perplexed. "If the brain is made up of people, then what the hell is in the Fourth Room of the Tetrons?"

"Nothing," the old man said in amusement.

"You're kidding me, right?" asked Ariel, incredulous.

"No, it's the truth. The Modelbyte T0 robots create the vacuum to build a gigantic version of the MEV that guarantees a constant power supply to the Tetron network."

"Gah, it's so frustrating!" Ariel protested. "All that time wasted, wondering what's in that damned room, just to discover there's nothing there!"

Once again, the world around him fell silent. Ariel now found himself lying in his bedroom in his parents' house.

Old Zimdar opened the door, and his voice was harsh. "No, young tyro, your time has not been wasted! The mystery of the Fourth Room symbolizes the faith that every citizen of Populana must have in democracy. Faith - although it might seem strange - is nourished by questions and by doubts, just like the ones you had when you were a child before you fell asleep at night."

"Sorry, but I don't understand how some kid thinking there might be an enormous dinosaur in the Fourth Room can help democracy," he objected. "It sounds like a contradiction to me. But isn't faith the *absence* of doubt?"

"Not so," Zimdar replied. "The decision to believe always comes from our uncertainty as to the possible answers to the questions we are asking. Having faith means embracing one of those answers without the certainty that it is correct. Therefore, we can say that faith also comes from doubt."

"Forgive me, but I still don't get it," Ariel interrupted him. "What does this have to do with the mystery of the Tetrons?"

His mentor spoke patiently. "We have said that believing is a choice between different answers, but the solutions to our question are not all the same. That in which we believe determines what we can build from it. You see, young tyro, a wise man chooses what to believe in based on what that act of faith allows him to do. And to do so, he examines all the possible alternatives. In our specific case, questioning the workings of democracy is a necessary step towards believing in it. Let me give you an example. Imagine that a certain drop of water considers itself superior to all the others, and believes it can create an ocean wave all by itself. It does not matter how strong its conviction is - it is still a single drop of water, destined to be carried along by the water that surrounds it. The only way in which that microscopic entity can shape its own path is to trust the drops that surround it, and to have the same intention as the others. But you see, that minuscule part of the whole will never understand the necessity of this step if it is denied the chance to try to move by itself. Its faith in the other drops comes precisely because it is *allowed* to verify that without the others it will never succeed in going anywhere. If we were not able to doubt democracy, we human beings could never understand why we must believe in it, and we would simply be dinosaurs, awaiting the next meteorite..."

"Thanks very much!" Ariel joked. "I feel a bit better now!"

Zimdar smiled and added "You should also consider that the vacuum inside the Fourth Room has a very practical purpose - it guarantees a constant supply of energy and the survival of the minds of the people who are no longer with us. When the power supply is interrupted, the flow of consciousness can continue to bounce between the Tetrons, to ensure this precious legacy is not lost forever."

"This is amazing!" Ariel breathed. "Basically, those people survive beyond death and are still contributing to determining the fate of society."

"That is correct. Life begins in the Tetrons, but does not end in them. It continues in the community, and when you connect to it, your mind renews that continuous flow of impulses, becoming part of this enormous brain. The experience is very pleasant, and this makes you want to come back, and so the cycle continues on and on forever. This enormous quantity of signals runs through the electrical grid and unites us all in a single sentient entity."

"Cool! And this collective mind interacts with us through the Great Network of the Tetrons," Ariel concluded, bringing his reasoning full circle.

The scene changed again, and Ariel found himself with Joe Plum once more, in what he assumed was the handyman's home: the apartment was strewn with electrical parts and gadgets of all kinds.

"Precisely," Joe said. "The wireless signals from the Tetrons are an electromagnetic version of those that travel through the nervous system of a human being, permitting him to interact with the outside world. And this is where Razor comes in. By way of analogy, it's as if someone modified the impulses going to and from your brain. They determine what your eyes see, and the commands you give your body. If someone systematically changed these signals, you wouldn't realize a thing: your brain would remain intact, but some of the data stored in it might be corrupted. As far as the financial statements are concerned, for example, imagine having a piece of data in your memory, but every time you try to put it down on paper, your hands write something different. Now imagine that even when you try to read that piece of data somewhere else, you keep getting the same bit of wrong information. If this problem repeats itself uniformly over time, that error will become part of your memory without you even realizing it. This is what Razor did with its network of devices, and it's the very reason that you, Ariel Nat, are here now."

"What do you mean?" Ariel asked, confused.

"Well, lucky for us, Razor took a while to develop this system. At the beginning, the altered signals weren't perfectly synchronized throughout Populana, and we became aware of small discrepancies that lasted for around a minute. The Tetron of Novardia in particular, being close to Razor's headquarters, picked up the biggest anomalies. During this initial phase, it was easy to restore the data by cross-checking it with the different areas of Populana. Just before you got the Call, however, Razor had improved the system to the point that the anomalies lasted just a few milliseconds. Even though these imperfections were still manageable, the power needed to cope with them began to exceed the capacity of the electrical grid…".

"The famous power outages!" Ariel broke in.

"Bingo! When we realized we were losing our battle, we knew we had to change strategy, so we decided to save a large portion of the data in your brain, so we could recover it once Razor was out of the game. Obviously, that's not what the Kurmar VR chairs are designed to do, hence the nasty burn on your neck…"

"Why choose me?" Ariel asked curiously.

"Who knows?" Joe smiled. "If I asked you to pick a number from one to five million, you'd have a hard time explaining why you chose the number you did. Maybe there was a reason, deep down, but you wouldn't know what it was. The same went for us."

"Good to know it's nothing personal when a meteorite hits you on the head," Ariel joked.

Joe burst into peals of laughter before turning into Zimdar once more. This time they were in an archive, which Ariel supposed was the old man's previous place of employment at the university.

"The saving of the data in your brain and the burn on your neck were events that were somehow foreseen by the founding fathers. They probably feared that something like this would happen, due to the natural predisposition of certain individuals to prevaricate over others."

"When it comes down to it, they didn't really have all that much faith in humanity," Ariel said wryly.

"My young tyro, faith in the majority of men should not be confused with faith in all men. If you release a wolf among a flock of lambs, he will kill every one. A democratic society prepares its defenses, but it must never forget that the wolves are always there, scrabbling at the fences. It must always be on the alert, because certain battles need to be fought and won every day."

"In this case, though, it seems to me like you've lost a lot of those battles, starting with the one for management of the electrical grid. Baiting Mandeo like that wasn't such a great idea."

"If we had won the auction before Razor managed to modify the financial statements, we would have been successful on two fronts: putting the network into safe hands, and increasing the production of energy when we needed it most. Unfortunately, this risk did not pay off, given that Razor got there before us, managing to synchronize its signals perfectly before making its offer. You know what they say: if you do not control your money, it controls you. In any case, that error triggered a series of events that have led us here today, with the Razor network on its knees."

"Right," agreed Ariel. "We were incredibly lucky! If I think back over all the crossroads in this whole story, and the number of things that seemed to go wrong but then fell into place... for example, what would've happened if I hadn't accepted the Call? If I hadn't had Zimdar as a mentor? If I'd never crashed into Sara in the supermarket? If I hadn't hated Charlie

Baid? If I hadn't met Joe Plum? If Karen Tanf hadn't been fired? If I'd never flooded my apartment?"

The scene changed again.

"You're right," interrupted the girl sitting in front of the armored tank. "That's a lot of coincidences. Apart from the choice to put you in that cell, and various other details we were able to control, the rest is pretty surprising. And believe me, all of us have thought about it for a long time," she said, pointing to the people sitting in the circle around the fire.

The girl got up and went over to the tank. "How would history have gone if this gun hadn't jammed that day? Why didn't the shot leave the chamber? Why did Roger Mann try to destroy this chunk of metal with his bare hands? Why didn't I kill him? I could have done it easily. Why did the Great War spare the Chandaha university library and all the other tools that allowed us to rebuild civilization in just fifty years? Why did the survivors join us? All facts with no logical explanation. And not only those. If you think about it, the world of today wouldn't even exist without the men like Latropp, who almost destroyed humanity with their insatiable thirst for power. And we owe a debt of recognition even to those people who lived politics like fans in a stadium, and who fought each other to the delight of those who exploited them."

"With all those brains and all that time at your disposal, you must have worked out who it is that moves the strings of our existence and why they do it," Ariel broke in.

"No, my canny friend. There *is* no reason for all this, just we ourselves who give a meaning to events. Things happen by chance; they have no intrinsic sig-

199

nificance. They happen, and that's that. It's our reactions as human beings that give substance to events. It's this instinct that steers history, and allows us to overcome adversity. It's thanks to this strength of ours, and to reason itself that we're all still breathing. And so, young man, do not seek the answers in other dimensions or in abstract entities. Look for them inside your own humanity, and in that of the people around you, because *that* is the secret of our existence. Each man lives in the people he encounters, and in those they go on to meet, a continuous exchange that defines humanity in its entirety. And so, Ariel Nat, love, hate if you wish, but do not forget that you are part of something bigger. And that deep down, the only real purpose of life is to live, to nourish this constant flow of consciousness that binds all men in a single destiny..."

At that precise instant, a blinding white flash split the sky, and the whole world was extinguished in a rainbow of colors.

49. RESURRECTION

"Is he still alive?" Sara asked in concern, dusting herself off.

"It seems so, he is still breathing," Zimdar said, bending over him to check.

"Whoa, that was some blast!" exclaimed Joe. "The technicians at Kurmar'll have their work cut out trying to sort this mess out!"

At that moment, Ariel regained consciousness - his neck ached, and his nostrils prickled with the stink of burnt quantum processor.

"Oh no, not again!" he thought, opening his eyes. "This is getting ridiculous!"

It took him a while to focus, but all he could see was a mass of whitish filaments. He sniffed to see what it was, but regretted it immediately, because it stank like a sewer.

Shifting his gaze, he realized it was Zimdar, bending over him to see if he was still alive.

"Dammit old man, you know I care about you, but you can forget about a kiss! My lips were hoping for something a little sweeter..." he joked, straightening his back and winking at Sara.

"Ariel!" the three yelled in delight, throwing themselves on to him in a collective embrace, where they lingered, cradled in that happiness, snug in a wordless joy that had the sound of their breathing, until the opening of the Tetron brought them back to their senses.

"We'd better get out of here," Joe warned. "The technicians will soon reconnect the power supply, and we don't want to be here when it happens. You, Ariel, have to go back to your cell, and I have to close the passageway we used, otherwise we'll all be sharing your cell before the night's over."

"You are right," Zimdar agreed, fighting back his curiosity. "Let us go, you can tell us all about it later."

They stepped warily out of the pyramid, preparing to flee, but there was no need.

The scene was horrific. Kostas, mortally wounded, had used the last of his strength to shoot Mandeo twice in the chest, before the High Representative had collapsed on top of him. They had died together, just as they had lived over the last few months, bound by the same destiny.

"Come on," Zimdar said sadly, "there is nothing we can do for them."

They soon reached the car and sped back through the streets of Allesia to the manhole they had come out of.

"You will forgive me if I do not accompany you this time," Zimdar said, apologetically.

Joe nodded in agreement. "There's no need. Ariel will help me close the passageway."

Ariel gazed longingly at Sara: he detested the idea

of leaving her again.

She leaned in close and whispered in his ear. "Whatever happens, Ariel Nat, this isn't a farewell, just a goodbye. I'll come and visit you every day of your sentence if that's what it takes, but nothing will ever keep me away from you again!"

It was a matter of seconds. Each one's gaze seemed to see into the heart of the other, and their lips, as if drawn together by an invisible force, met in a passionate kiss.

"My dearest lovebirds... shall we go, or shall we wait for the guards to bring you breakfast in bed?" Zimdar teased.

Ariel caressed Sara's cheek one last time before diving back into the sewer.

50. FREEDOM

Going back to his cell wasn't easy. As dawn approached, the flow of slime in the waste pipe grew thicker, progress was slow, and the two were relieved that Zimdar was not with them.

Heaving himself through the hole in the wall required him to call on all the training he had done in prison, not to mention the half-dozen shirts he sweated through to in his efforts to seal up the passageway, under the stern supervision of the old Forgez wizard in dungarees.

When he had finished, he took a never-ending shower, and when the guard came with his breakfast, it was pretty embarrassing having to pretend he'd soiled himself to get a change of clothes and clean sheets.

Luckily that was the last unpleasant event of the day, and it wasn't long before things fell back into place at an impressive rate.

Reading the news that morning, Ariel learned of a strange power outage and the discovery of two bodies near the entrance of the Tetron of Allesia. The two men, Mandeo Gutt and Kostas Bull, both High Representatives, had killed each other.

Although their motives were unknown, it was thought that they were connected to the sabotage of the Kurmar VR chair, found exploded inside the pyramid, or to matters relating to the political activity of the two men.

A zealous inspector, to find out more, had checked the recent paperwork of the two Representatives, and had ordered an investigation into all the companies which had participated in the auction promoted by Mandeo.

Although nothing relevant to the investigation had yet emerged, the financial checks had shown that Razor was in the red by 860 million schlepps, far in excess of the threshold of forced bankruptcy. And so, the company had been put under temporary receivership, effective immediately, and the State had taken control of it to sell its assets and pay its creditors. As if that wasn't enough, the police who had gone to Villa Larvini to question the brothers about the company's books had found it deserted: the two had vanished into thin air.

Later that morning, Ariel also heard the announcement by the High Chamber that management of the electrical company would go to the second highest bidder at the auction - Kurmar Enterprise, which had passed all the checks with flying colors.

But the good news for Ariel did not end there. The sum credited to his account by Novalit United had disappeared, and his request for an appeal was accepted immediately.

When his new lawyer, Brandi Gicer, called him to

tell him about the review of his trial set for the late afternoon, her tone was reassuring. "The evidence used to sentence you no longer exists. Tonight you'll be having dinner in your High Representative's lodgings, guaranteed!"

And so it was: the three judges could do nothing other than acknowledge the strange judicial error and annul his sentence.

On hearing of the revocation of his sentence, Ariel was unable to contain his delight. Being deprived of his freedom had shown him just how important it was, and he vowed never to waste another moment of his life.

It was in this mood of elation that he rushed into his lodgings to call Sara. But there was no need. She was already there, and their joy erupted into tender gestures of affection.

After a brief dinner prepared by Sara, they decided to spend the rest of the evening in bed, in a never-ending exchange of words, gazes, silences and caresses, both of them rediscovering the true meaning of the word love.

51. HEROES

Ariel woke at six thirty. Sara was still asleep beside him.

He lay there for a moment, watching her. The first light of dawn filtering through the window illuminated her skin, in an interplay of light and shadows that highlighted her curves.

But that was not why he was admiring her. When one of them had needed help, the other one had been there. They had supported each other, taken risks, and fought for a greater good. And that night they had joined together in a single body and a single mind. Never in his life had he felt so close to someone.

He got up and went into the kitchen. It was exactly seven o'clock in the morning, but the silence seemed surreal somehow.

"Of course, that's what's missing! Zimdar's ring at the door!" Ariel thought, as his thoughts ran nostalgically to his first few days at the High Chamber of Populana.

And so, the first thing he did after breakfast was call Joe and Zimdar, to organize a trip to Chandaha that evening.

"Why Chandaha?" his old mentor asked.

"Sara and I thought it would be the most appropriate place for what we want to tell you," Ariel replied before he left for work.

When Ariel had finished at the Chamber that day, the party left Allesia, arriving at the ruins of Chandaha towards dusk.

The sun was going down. "Come on, let's make a fire. It'll be cold soon," Ariel said.

In front of the armored tank, he made a circle of stones, collected some firewood from under the big tree, and added a few firelighters he had bought at the supermarket.

The fire began crackling almost immediately, as if impatient to get started, and the four of them sat down to enjoy that gentle warmth.

Sara spoke first. "The story I'm about to tell you has been handed down through my family for generations. It's something very personal, but I've decided to tell it to you, because after everything we've been through together, you're like brothers to me."

And she began telling the secret she had revealed to her beloved Ariel just weeks before.

When she had finished, it was Ariel's turn to describe in detail his incredible experience during those fifteen minutes when the Tetron was downloading the data from his mind.

After his final words were lost among the streets of Chandaha, the four remained in silence for a while, all reflecting on those marvelous revelations, and if it hadn't been for the crackling of the fire, they would have heard the orchestra of their thoughts.

Zimdar was the first to break the silence. "Do you think we should tell the public about our adventure?"

"Sara and I talked about it last night," Ariel replied. "If you agree, we think we should leave things be. We want to follow the example of the soldiers who founded Populana. Hand the story down to our children and no-one else."

Joe let out a sigh. "But that would mean denying Populana its heroes once again. You could be a source of inspiration for future generations."

"I pity the society that needs heroes to survive!" Ariel said.

Then he explained. "Kings. Heroes. Geniuses. Leaders. Messiahs. They're just words used to hide what really moves the history of humanity. Short-sighted people who let their own name obscure those of the others who contributed to their success. Where would the great knight be without his squires or his enemies? Could a king even exist without his people? A leader without militants? A messiah without disciples to carry his good word to all corners of the Earth? Where would the great scientist be without the work of all those who have written books and perpetuated knowledge until he came on the scene? And where would *we* be without Karen Tanf, Charlie Baid, Toss Sterling, Ortiep Nob, Marianne Giltor, Coss Molo, Tom Maz, Tim Coan, Mandeo Gutt, Kostas Bull, the Larvini brothers, the founding fathers and all the people who over centuries have lived in Populana and on the Earth? Nowhere, that's where, because history is written by all humans together, and heroes are just names, labels that we stick on it to twist it and distort it. They deform it, creating the illusion that it's individuals who bring about change. No, my dear Joe, heroes are nothing but a mirage, the image of the world reflected in the broken mirror of the ego, showing a single person where it should instead be showing many, many more. Believe us, Populana will be much better off without heroes."

They all looked at each other for a moment, before getting to their feet, one by one. Sara took Ariel's hand, and Ariel took Joe's, who in turn took the hand of Zimdar, until the circle closed as Sara took the old man's hand in hers.

And so, as those few surviving soldiers had done centuries before, they solemnly swore to reveal that story to their own children and to no-one else, as the fire began to fade, and darkness fell to cover that bleak armored tank once more.

I would like to thank my partner, my family, my friends, colleagues, and all the people I have met in my life.

All of them have contributed to writing this book.

Andrea Meneghini

Andrea Meneghini

This book exists thanks to your support.
If you liked it, please leave a review.

If you wish to contact me, you can reach me at
andrea.meneghini.books@outlook.com

25171075R00124

Printed in Great Britain
by Amazon